The Secret to Lying

TODD MITCHELL

CANDLEWICK PRESS

Copyright © 2010 by Todd Mitchell

First edition 2010

Library of Congress Cataloging-in-Publication Data

Mitchell, Todd.
The secret to lying / Todd Mitchell. — 1st ed.
p. cm.
Summary: Fifteen-year-old James lies about himself to be considered "cool" when
he gets into an exclusive boarding school, but soon unnaturally vivid dreams of
being a demon-hunting warrior lead to self-destructive acts while he is awake.
ISBN 978-0-7636-4084-2
[1. Popularity — Fiction. 2. Honesty — Fiction. 3. Self-actualization
(Psychology) — Fiction. 4. Boarding schools — Fiction. 5. High schools — Fiction.
6. Schools — Fiction. 7. Dreams — Fiction. 8. Demonology — Fiction.] I. Title.
PZ7.M6955Sec 2010
[Fic] — dc22   2009032484

10 11 12 13 14 15 MVP 10 9 8 7 6 5 4 3 2 1

Printed in York, PA, U.S.A.

This book was typeset in Warnock.

Candlewick Press
99 Dover Street
Somerville, Massachusetts 02144

visit us at www.candlewick.com

For Kerri, my ghost and more

PROLOGUE

People often ask how I got these scars. There are several slashes along my right arm; faint scratches on my back; a few large scars, thick as leeches, on my shoulders; and a few more on my legs. It looks like I've been wrestling tigers or battling samurai. I'm a street fighter. A rebel. A real badass.

At least that's the story I sometimes try to suggest.

Sometimes I answer their questions with a different story. I tell people the folktale I once heard about the old witch who eats all your scars when you die, and if you don't have enough scars to feed her, she eats out your eyes, leaving you blind in the next world. I tell them I want to be sure that won't happen to me.

But if I'm going to be honest, then I can't do it in a half-assed way. I have to admit the embarrassing stuff, and the bad stuff, and the stuff I wish I hadn't done.

The truth is, I got these scars fighting demons.

That's the short version.

Here's the long.

Part I

We are such stuff
As dreams are made on, and our little life
Is rounded with a sleep.

— *THE TEMPEST*, ACT 4, SCENE 1

Me

I WAS THE GUY no one noticed.

Case in point: during my freshman year, I went out for football. It wasn't difficult to make the team—my hometown high school was so small that they barely cut anyone. I didn't suck at football, but I wasn't great at it, either. The only reason I kept playing was because Kinsey Jackson, the girl I'd had a crush on since kindergarten, cheered on the pep squad. Then, as if fate conspired to bring us together, Kinsey drew my locker number for Spirit Week.

It was supposed to be a secret, which pep squad girl had drawn our locker number, but Ginny Goodman told me because she knew I had a thing for Kinsey. For days I imagined what Kinsey might do to my locker to psych me up for the Homecoming Game. I even wrote her a thank-you letter that I planned on slipping into her locker afterward. The letter was three pages long and ended by asking her to the Homecoming Dance. I pictured her running up to me with pages in hand and whispering *Yes*.

When I got to school the next day, the lockers of all the football players were decorated with glittery red *H*'s for *Huskies,* our mascot. Some players, like Dave McEwan, got four or five *H*'s on their lockers, along with bags of homemade cookies. Guys clamored in the halls, bragging about their decorations while stealing treats from each other.

I hurried to my locker, eager to see what Kinsey had done for me, but there was nothing.

No *H*.

No streamers.

No cookies.

I looked on the floor in case my *H* had fallen off. Then I looked around in case someone had taken my cookies as a joke. That's when I noticed Kinsey flirting with Dave McEwan at the end of the hall.

It's no big deal, I told myself. There are kids who are orphaned, or shipwrecked, or fighting in wars—every story we read in English class focused on someone coping with something big. Compared to their problems, not getting an *H* was definitely not worth talking about. But that was the problem. Nothing in my life was worth talking about. I was so unremarkable that no one even noticed I'd been forgotten.

The rest of my freshman year drifted by in pretty much the same way. I didn't try out for any other sports or write any more letters to girls I liked. I just coasted through my classes, dreaming of a different life. And maybe I would have gone on like that forever if Principal Kay hadn't called me into her office a few weeks before the school year ended.

She told me to sit and flipped through my file, which didn't take long. There couldn't have been much in it to read, other than some test scores, records of my crappy attendance, and an uninspired grade point average.

"I don't get it," she said.

"Am I in trouble?" I asked.

"That depends, James. What are you doing here?"

"Nothing," I said.

"I see that." She shook her head and frowned. "Your test scores aren't bad."

"Tests are easy."

"Really?" Principal Kay gave me a long look.

I fidgeted, not knowing what she wanted me to say. Did she think I'd cheated or something?

She sifted through a pile of papers on her desk, pulled out a glossy brochure, and handed it to me. "Any chance you might be interested in this?"

I studied the cover. *Discover your potential. . . .* was written above a picture of a kid pouring liquid into a beaker. Along the bottom, in large block letters, it said THE AMERICAN SCIENCE AND MATHEMATICS ACADEMY. According to the brochure, ASMA was "the state's premier high school for academically gifted students." In other words, a refuge for geeks.

I looked at Principal Kay, confused about why she'd given the brochure to me. Science and math weren't my favorite subjects, and I definitely wasn't "gifted." I didn't consider myself very geeky, either. Sure, I'd scored well on standardized tests and I got decent grades, but classes at my small-town high school were a joke.

"You never know what you're capable of until you try, James," Principal Kay said.

I shrugged.

"No one from this school has applied before," she added.

That caught my attention. "Why not?"

"I suppose other qualified students didn't want to live away from home."

I flipped through the brochure again, noticing the dorms in the background of one of the pictures. The campus was more than two hours away. "I'd have to live there?"

"It's one of the only public residential high schools in the country," she said. "Quite a unique opportunity."

On my way back to class, I walked past the pictures of all the varsity football teams for the past fifty years or so. I stopped at my dad's picture. He was in the third row, second from the end, not smiling. He might have been trying to look tough, but instead he seemed nervous.

I followed the pictures to the end of the hall, where my team picture would eventually hang. The years blurred together into diluted red and tan squares. Uniforms and hairstyles changed, but the players looked the same. At the beginning of the year, Coach Wayne had told us that we should be proud to be part of such a great tradition. The funny thing was, our football team had never been that great. We were barely even average.

And then there was me—among the average, I was no one.

Everyone in my town had known me for so long, there was no way to get them to see that they didn't really know me at all. To them, I was just the quiet guy who sat behind them in math class. The one who didn't get an *H* and never said anything about it. The sort of guy no one told stories about.

At least that's who I used to be.

I took home the application and filled it out.

FreSH STaRt

MOMS TRIED TO HELP ME decorate my room.

"Honey, you don't want to put this up," she said, holding a ripped and faded Sid Vicious poster. "Let's get you something to brighten the place—flowers, or a landscape, or something in a frame." She looked at the poster and wrinkled her nose. "I'm going to throw this away."

I rolled my eyes, refusing to lose it in front of Richard, call-me-Dickie, the roommate I'd met only five minutes before. We'd talked once on the phone over the summer, after the administration had sent me a sheet with his phone number on it and the suggestion that we coordinate furnishings. All I knew about Dickie was that he'd bring the minifridge.

Dickie stuffed socks into the dresser on his side of the room, pretending not to notice the growing tension.

"It's his room," my dad said. "Let him decorate how he likes."

Moms turned to Dickie. "What do you think, Richard?" she asked, waving the poster around. "Do you want *this* hanging in your room?"

Dickie looked from Moms to me. "Don't encourage her," I said.

"Sure, Mrs. Turner," Dickie replied. "I think it adds a certain reckless, down-and-out pastiche."

Pastiche?

Moms smiled at Dickie. "So grunge is in?"

"Sid isn't grunge," I interrupted, embarrassed by her desperate attempt to sound cool. "He's punk."

"Whatever. He's grungy-looking, isn't he?" she asked, addressing Dickie again.

"Definitely grungy," Dickie agreed. "But what can you do? Girls go crazy for that sort of thing."

"Really?"

"Oh, yeah, Mrs. Turner. It's all part of the bad-boy mystique."

Moms smiled, charmed by my blond, blue-eyed roommate. "I see. Then I guess we'll have to put it up."

She tacked the poster to the wall and, with Dickie's encouragement, arranged some of our other furnishings — stringing up the Christmas lights I'd brought and designing a study corner with a lava lamp. My roommate complimented her on her sophisticated sense of taste and style.

"You're too sweet," Moms said, basking in the praise.

Dickie winked at me. Even though his schmoozing annoyed me, I was still relieved to be rooming with him. Most of the other students I'd seen moving in had stunned me with their nerdliness—skinny arms, big glasses, buck teeth, stringy hair . . . the works.

My dad fiddled with the shades on the windows while Moms surveyed the room. "What else should we do?" she asked. "Curtains? Do you need curtains? I think there are some stores down the road."

"I don't need curtains," I replied.

"What about making your bed?"

"I'm almost sixteen. I think I can handle it."

"Hey, James," Dad called. He snapped a picture as I turned. The flash stung my eyes. "Got you." He slid the camera back into his shirt pocket and checked his watch. "Well, it's getting late."

"I'll walk you out," I offered.

Moms sighed, acting dramatic. "Fine. If you don't want us here."

"It was wonderful meeting you, Mr. and Mrs. Turner," Dickie said.

She squeezed his hand and gave him one of her radiant fake smiles. "You take care of my boy, now," she said to Dickie, as if she were giving me up for adoption.

I hurried them through the hall to keep Moms from talking with anyone else. Dad thumped the walls and remarked about the quality of the construction. "You're lucky to have a bathroom in every room," he said. "Most college dorms aren't this nice."

I nodded and kept walking. It was always the same with them—Moms needing to be the center of attention while Dad slouched around in his wrinkled work shirts, muttering about particleboard and car engines.

Outside, the parking lot swarmed with parents carrying grocery bags full of ramen and soda and other last-minute "necessities" snagged from the store. A few kids, standing with their parents beside a minivan or an SUV, seemed to be crying. Moms dabbed her eyes like she might cry, too, although I doubted she would. She just loved scenes.

"We could get you some snacks," she said. "Don't you need snacks?"

"I'm fine."

"Maybe more granola bars?"

"I have plenty."

Moms pouted. "I bet other kids would be happy to have their mom get them snacks."

I stayed silent, trying not to argue with her.

Dad jingled the car keys. "Let's go, Hannah."

She sighed and hugged me good-bye. Then she got in the car and flipped down the mirror to fix her mascara.

Dad paused before opening the driver's door. "James," he called.

I met his tired, sagging eyes. We were exactly the same height, but with his round shoulders and slight belly, he looked shorter. He rubbed the stubble on his cheek. "James," he repeated. "Listen. Always keep a spare roll of toilet paper in your closet. If the one in the bathroom runs out, it's good to know where an extra can be found."

"Sure," I said, not certain how to respond to this gem of fatherly wisdom.

He nodded and shook my hand, then we hugged, awkwardly slapping each other's backs.

I watched the car pull away. Moms waved, wiggling her fingers. Dad drove slowly out of the parking lot, signaled, and turned onto the main road. The drab gray back of the car receded, disappearing behind rows of corn.

And that was it—I was free. I imagined jumping into the air and shouting like at the end of some cheesy high-school flick where a graduate in a robe tosses his cap and the camera freezes on it and no one knows what happens afterward. Except I wasn't graduating. Here I was, only a high-school sophomore, already on my own.

The possibilities seemed endless. I could go back to my room and unpack, or dump my clothes onto the floor and kick them under the bed. Swig a two-liter of Coke. Wrap myself in toilet paper. Get a tattoo. Change my name. . . . All the strings were cut. No one here knew me, so no one could hold me back.

My life had finally started.

Trust Fall

IT STARTED WITH A LIE.

During the first four days, sophomores were required
to do a variety of orientation activities. There were six
dorms at ASMA—three girls' dorms and three boys'.
Each dorm had four wings, laid out in an X with a kitchen
and computer lab in each wing and a commons in the
center. All the dorms together looked like a line of chro-
mosomes about to divide.

I lived in D wing, otherwise known as Dingo wing.
This was written in Magic Marker above the door to our
wing. Mike, our Resident Counselor—a thirtysomething
bald guy with so much hair on his chest it puffed out his
shirt—made us all attend a wing party after the parents
left on Thursday so Dingo-wingers could "bond." He gave

us chips and soda, and interview forms we were supposed to fill out by questioning our roommates.

Dickie encouraged me to introduce him as the illegitimate child of Lord Scrotium, a famous British politician. Mike frowned while I elaborated on Dickie's lifelong ambition to be recognized by his father and reclaim the Scrotium lands, tower, and title.

"Well done, old chap!" Dickie said in a fake British accent. Then he introduced me as a Sid Vicious fan with pyromaniac tendencies. Apparently, I'd accidentally burned down my previous school and the principal had fudged my entrance exams so I could be foisted off on ASMA. I nodded, coolly going along with the joke.

If Dickie had given a purely factual introduction, it would have gone something like this: James Turner grew up in a cornfield, but his parents weren't farmers. His dad is a tractor parts salesman who fixes TVs in his spare time and pretty much lives in the basement. His mom, an ex–Homecoming Queen, calls herself an independent businesswoman, which means she sells lipstick for Avon. James is an only child, or rather, an accidental child, since his parents married out of circumstance (to put it politely). He's never traveled anyplace except Indiana and Wisconsin, both of which are more interesting than Illinois, but not by much. He once lit a whole matchbook on fire and singed his fingers. Other than that, he hasn't won any contests, burned down any buildings, or done anything remotely noteworthy.

Dickie's introduction was far more interesting. A few Dingo-wingers chuckled while stealing glances at me, as if they thought some of it might be real. I did my best to encourage this impression. Anything was better than the truth.

Following introductions, Chuck, the school counselor, dropped by our wing to talk with us. He was built like a linebacker, with wide, meaty shoulders and a scarred-up face—not the sort of guy you'd normally expect to lead a hug-in. Also, he was missing one eye and he didn't wear a patch or anything. He let the lid hang limp. I wondered what I'd see if he suddenly opened it. A pink, empty socket? A flat, milky eyeball? A hole to his brain? The thought of it grossed me out, but I couldn't stop staring.

Chuck gave this lecture about the pressures we'd encounter at ASMA, and the homesickness people might experience, and how we were each other's family now, so we had to look out for each other. "No one has to go through anything alone," he said. To illustrate this point, he had everyone do a trust-fall off a chair into the waiting arms of fellow Dingo-wingers. One kid was so floppy it was like catching a Muppet.

When it was my turn, I acted like the whole thing was too dumb to bother me. I fell back without flinching. It wasn't that I trusted everyone so much. It was that I'd already begun to see myself as a different person.

I closed my eyes and fell away from the dull nobody I used to be.

• ■ ■

Orientation activities continued for most of Friday and Saturday, ranging from tours of the campus to lectures on maintaining proper hygiene while living away from home. The upperclassmen called it "scorientation" and boasted about how easy sophomore girls were to hook up with. Since the school was only a three-year program, sophomores were the youngest. Essentially, we were the freshmen of the place. During breaks between sessions, I watched some of the junior and senior guys circling groups of sophs like hawks, trying to pick out the hotties.

Saturday night, we were required to attend a sophomore-only lock-in so our class could meet apart from the desperate upperclassmen. I walked with Dickie and his friend Heinous to the main complex. After signing in and stashing our pillows and toothbrushes in the auditorium, Dickie, Heinous, and I wandered the building looking for something to do. A few guys from our dorm were shooting hoops in the gym while some girls sat on the bleachers, talking. The guys tried to slam-dunk and do half-court shots, showing off, except none of them were very good.

"Here we have the rare, speckled pumpkin pusher," Heinous whispered, imitating the narrator on a wildlife show. "This particular subspecies is of the geekish-jock grouping, commonly known as jeeks. Notice how cunningly they fondle the ball."

Steve Lacone, a tall, well-built jeek who lived in Boomer wing, glared at us.

"Shh . . . we've been spotted," Heinous said. He ducked behind an imaginary shrub. "They're dangerous when females are present."

"I say," Dickie quipped in an exaggerated British accent, "no heckling the athletes."

"Right-o." Heinous popped out of the imaginary shrubs. "Carry on!" he shouted. "Pushy the pumpkin!"

Heinous and Dickie had known each other before ASMA. They both came from southern Illinois and had gone to school together, so they'd had years to polish their routines. In many ways, the two were polar opposites. Where Dickie was a pale-skinned smooth-talker, Heinous was a dark-complexioned, obnoxious spaz. I figured my place in the trio would be to play the quiet, brooding rebel.

Heinous continued his wildlife expedition as we left the gym to see what else was going on. "The yellow-bellied nerdling," he said, when we approached a group of skinny gamers in the hall. "Stay back!" he hissed, throwing out his arms. "There's a peculiar odor to this species."

One of the gamers rolled some dice and shouted "Yes!" while pumping his fist.

"That's part of their mating dance," Heinous whispered. "Perhaps, if we're lucky, they'll attempt to mount."

We wandered past the gamers to the art room, but a large number of "red-spotted mathletes" had gathered there for a *Star Wars* marathon. Then, in the photography room, Heinous spied a flock of "lesser poseur vampires," a species with an affinity for black, known to play dead when frightened.

In the cafeteria, we found a group of "Barbie wan-nabes" gossiping around a table. At one end sat the most beautiful girl I'd ever seen. Students at ASMA weren't exactly model material, but even at a normal school, she would have stood out. She looked like she'd stepped off a movie poster, with her waifish figure, wide smile, and blades of straight blond hair brushing her cheekbones.

"Who's that?" I asked.

Dickie raised his eyebrows. "Didn't you scan your facebook?"

"No," I said. "I skipped that assignment."

"Well, dear roomie, the supermodel is Ellie Frost."

"The Ice Queen," Heinous added.

"Definitely the Ice Queen," Dickie agreed.

Ellie glanced at us, then looked away. She didn't seem to be talking with anyone at the table. It was more like the other girls had gathered around her, as though simply being near her might make them popular.

"Whatever you're thinking, forget it," Dickie said. "It seems that the Ice Queen doesn't date sophomores."

"Really?"

"She's already going out with Mark Watson."

"Ah, yes," Heinous mused as we left the cafeteria, "one of the golden-crested senior thugs."

We made our way back to the auditorium. The main lights were off, but dim strings of orange lights ran along the bottom of each of the aisle steps. A few students huddled like refugees between seat rows, trying to sleep. A few others appeared to be faking sleep so they could make out, sheltered from the prying eyes of RCs policing the lock-in. I envied the couples, amazed by how quickly they'd hooked up. Except for one hurried lip-smooshing during a truth-or-dare game, I'd never even kissed a girl.

Dickie wove through the scattered bodies in the auditorium, cutting a path to the front. The curtain was open, and three girls sat onstage in a semicircle, the dim light barely illuminating their faces. I recognized one of them as Sunny Burke. Dickie had talked with her the night before at the ice-cream social while I stood silently nearby.

"The freckled puff," Heinous said as Dickie strolled toward Sunny. Her hair was tied back in two cute pigtails. "Notice her fine plumage," Heinous continued. "Watch as the male approaches, attempting to mount."

"The lonely wanker," Dickie replied. "This chattering species can be recognized by his tendency to spank his monkey."

The girls stopped talking when we approached. All three of them were barefoot and in pajamas.

"Ladies," Dickie said in true lounge-singer form, "what lovely outfits."

"Why, thank you," Sunny replied. "It's flannel—all the rage in Paris this year."

Sunny introduced Sage Fisher, her roommate, and

Katy Cameron. They scooted back so we could sit onstage with them. After introductions, Dickie and Heinous launched into a story about how they'd superglued everyone's locker shut at the end of their freshman year. Sunny, who had the prettiest laugh you ever heard, found the story hilarious. The cinnamon dash of freckles on her nose crinkled when she smiled.

Heinous's roommate, Cheese, joined our circle, and pretty soon everyone was sharing stories of where they'd come from and what they'd done before ASMA.

I sat back, listening, but not part of the group. Already things were starting to seem like they had at my old school. The guys tried to impress the girls, and the girls giggled nervously, egging them on, while I hovered around the outskirts, easily overlooked—the extra hired to form a crowd.

"What about you?" Sage asked.

It took a moment before I realized she meant me.

"What?"

"Do you miss home?"

"No." Everyone looked at me, expecting more of an answer. "Not much to miss. I grew up in a cornfield," I said. Their attention started to drift, already bored by my lame story. Dickie would have cracked a joke by now.

"That's why I used to run away a lot," I added. It wasn't true, but it could have been.

"You did?" Sage's eyes widened.

"Yup. I'd steal a car and drive all night trying to get to someplace interesting."

"You stole cars?"

"Well, I didn't really steal them," I explained. "It was more like *borrowing* cars, because I usually returned them."

"Hold on," Cheese said. "You can hot-wire a car?"

"Nope." I shrugged, like it was no big deal. "But if you look around on enough cars, you can usually find a spare key stashed somewhere."

"That's true," Dickie chimed in, saving me. "My parents tuck one inside the front bumper if you want to borrow the BMW."

"So where would you go?" Sage asked.

"North, usually, to Wisconsin," I said, surprised by how easily everyone seemed to believe me. "And once I tried to go to California, but after driving six hours, I ran out of gas money and had to hitchhike home."

"No shit?" Heinous asked.

"No shit," I replied. "There wasn't anything to do in my hometown except fight, and I got sick of that."

Sage looked concerned. "You used to get in fights?"

"Not angry fights," I said, trying to brush it off, but everyone kept looking at me. All of them were listening now, so I had to keep going—building the story, making it real. "I was part of a full-contact martial arts league."

"Like ultimate fighting?" Sage asked.

"A little. Except sometimes we used weapons."

"Dude, you're so full of crap," Heinous said. "Fight Club, my ass."

I pulled back my sleeve, exposing a thick, white scar on the inside of my forearm from an oven burn. "That's how I got this."

"Bloody hell!" Dickie sounded impressed. "I'll never take your Pop-Tarts."

Sage dragged her finger along the inside of my arm. "Did it hurt?"

"I don't fight anymore." I pulled my sleeve down over the scar. "That was the old me. Now I'm starting over."

"Wow," she said.

Sage and Sunny kept pressing me for details. The more they listened, the more I lied, laying the groundwork for the new me. James Turner: Reckless fighter. Pyromaniac. Delinquent. Troubled runaway who'd stolen cars and lived on the streets of Madison. If they believed only half the things I said, it would be enough.

Details poured out of me, sticking to the few lines of truth like snow on a branch. I may not have really run away, but I'd thought about it plenty of times, and I'd been to Madison. So why not rewrite the past? Truth was beauty, and beauty was truth.

The geeks let me be whatever I imagined.

The Ice Queen

THE SECRET TO LYING is this: believe yourself and others will believe you, too.

Rumors about me spread, spilling beyond the sophomore class. I repeated some of the stories I'd told at the lock-in and made up a few new ones, but mostly I acted modest, like my car-stealing, street-fighting past wasn't something I enjoyed talking about. Instead of bragging, I sounded like the sole survivor of a catastrophe, reluctantly giving an interview.

When classes started, I played up my bad-boy image by sitting in the back and perfecting a look of unimpressed boredom. Most of the students at ASMA were so used to being the star pupil, raising their hands to answer every question, that being quiet made me seem rebellious.

The one flaw in my plan was physics. Somehow, I'd scored well enough on the placement exams to be put in the advanced section. Only twelve sophomores were in Advanced Physics, so there was little chance of not participating. The class was populated by hard-core geeks like the Tanada twins (who were so freakishly smart that they'd both been recruited by the government to keep them from hacking into military systems), Jesus John (who wore his bathrobe to class and had hair down to his hips), Muppet (the floppy kid from Dingo wing), Angie Turkle (who announced on the first day that her goal in life was to be a "space surgeon"), Ninety (called such because he spoke at least ninety words a minute), Frank Wood (who actually parted his hair with a comb), and Cheese (the guy who roomed with Heinous, ate Cheetos constantly, and resembled a scruffy koala bear with thick glasses). There were a few other students I didn't know anything about, and then there was Ellie Frost, the Ice Queen.

At first, being in Advanced Physics with Ellie made me want to puke in my shoe. It went against every principle of fairness that she could be beautiful and smart to boot, but there she was, sitting at the front of the room, getting the answers right when Dr. Choi called on her. All class long, I'd steal glances at Ellie, and every time I saw her, my pulse would speed up and my head would spin. Then Dr. Choi would call on me, and I'd drop my pen or kick my desk while I stammered out an answer in a shaky voice because I couldn't stop worrying about what Ellie thought of me.

In order to function, I had to pretend that she wasn't there. I started arriving early to class so I could take the back corner desk, farthest from where Ellie sat. She never looked at me when she entered, and I tried not to look at her. Luckily, Frank Wood, the guy with the perfect part in his hair, helped keep me distracted. "Hey, James!" he'd say, practically shouting my name when he saw me. "What's going on?"

Frank sounded like an announcer from the 1950s. He usually hung out at my desk before class. We weren't exactly friends. It was more like he admired me. He'd been homeschooled, believed everything he heard, and seemed to think I was the most daring person he'd ever met. I tried not to disappoint.

"Is it true?" he asked one day in his booming, all-American voice.

I raised my head slightly, as if I had far more important things on my mind but I was willing to humor him. "Is what true?"

"Did you really light a baseball diamond on fire?" Frank's eyebrows arched.

I glanced toward the front of the room. Fortunately, Dr. Choi hadn't arrived yet. Only a couple other students, including the Ice Queen, were around. A lock of Ellie's hair brushed the corner of her mouth as she pulled her books out of her backpack. She didn't turn to look at me, but by the way her back stiffened, I suspected she was listening. "Who told you that?" I asked cryptically.

"Some guys in my wing were talking about it," Frank said. "Did it burn down?"

"No. It was beautiful."

Frank gave a nervous chuckle. "Beautiful?"

"Yeah." I glanced at Ellie again. She opened a folder and tapped her pencil against her cheek, pretending to work.

Frank kept asking me questions, so I told him about how my friend Dave McEwan and I spent weeks swiping gas and oil cans from open garages, until one night we mixed it all together and poured it over the baseball fence. Then I ran the bases while pouring gas from two five-gallon cans. Only, right as I rounded second, Dave tossed a match.

"What happened?" Frank asked.

Ellie stopped tapping her pencil against her cheek.

"I kept running," I said. "Dave shouted, 'Drop the cans!' but I didn't—not until I touched home plate. Then I chucked the cans against the backstop and the whole thing exploded into this huge fireball that spread around the outfield. It burned so bright everyone in town must have seen it."

"Holy cow!" Frank said. "Did you get caught?"

I shrugged. "Three cop cars and a fire truck came, but the fence was metal and the baseball diamond was sand, so there was nothing to put out. It was just beautiful."

At the end of class, Frank retold some of my story to Cheese. He sounded like a baseball fan recounting a great play. Even though he got some of the details wrong, I didn't bother correcting him. I was too distracted by Ellie. She gathered her books and headed for the door. Before she left, her eyes flicked over me.

The look she gave me sent a jolt up my spine. It wasn't interest, or curiosity, or worry. Instead, it was something more intense, like anger.

Who was I to be looking at the Ice Queen?

FReaKiNG

DICKIE STARTED GOING OUT with Sunny, which meant she was always in our room. The two of them mauled each other constantly. I tried to be happy for them, but seeing them together made me feel more lonely.

"I think I'll dye my hair," I said one day after busting in on them. The blankets on Dickie's bed were all messed up, yet Sunny insisted that they'd only been doing their homework and I should stick around.

"Purple," I mused, figuring I needed to do something drastic. "Or bright green."

"Purple," Sunny said. "Definitely purple."

"You think?" Dickie countered, studying me. "It wouldn't be too . . . Barney?"

Sunny shook her head. "No way. Dark purple would look hot on him."

"Hey, now." Dickie pretended to be jealous.

"Yup. You have to go purple," Sunny decided.

"I don't know."

"I'll help you with it," she offered. "It'll be fun."

I couldn't think of a way to back out without seeming chicken. "Okay. Dark purple it is," I said. "But nothing Barneyish."

Sunny begged a ride off her RC the next day so we could go to the nearest drugstore and buy supplies. The closest color to dark purple on offer was "Tropical Burgundy." I wanted to forget it then, but Sunny promised that no one would know the difference.

We had to get a pass before Sunny could come with me to my room. She showed me how to bleach my hair to make the dye show better. Then she bleached some streaks into her own hair with the leftover paste. Instead of coming out blond, my hair turned bright orange. I left a few clumps that way while coloring the rest. Sunny experimented with using cherry Kool-Aid on a lock of her hair. The color wasn't great, but it smelled delicious.

"Badass," she said when my hair was done.

I almost didn't recognize myself. After Sunny left, I kept glancing at my purple and orange-streaked hair, trying to get used to it.

Dickie seemed impressed by my new do when he saw it later. "Smashing," he said. "Your parents are going to love that."

"I aim to please."

Not to be outdone, he drew a fake eyelash beneath his eye and put on the black bowler hat that looked dumb on everyone else but cool on him. He was the spitting image of Alex DeLarge in *A Clockwork Orange*. "Tonight we freak," Dickie announced. Then he called Heinous and told him to prepare.

The whole point of freaking was not to fit in. Since ASMA was a three-year program, we'd all served our time as froshbait at some normal high school where kids would either ignore us or stuff us into lockers for being different. But here, among the smart kids, it was cool to be different.

I gelled my purple and orange-streaked hair into classic punk spikes while Heinous went for more of a deranged samurai look, putting his long black hair into a topknot and stuffing a broken broomstick into his belt for a sword. As soon as study hours ended, we grabbed a couple cans of shaving cream for mischief and headed out. The night air simmered with the sound of cicadas enjoying their last bit of summer warmth. People in shorts and T-shirts poured out of the dorms. After nearly three weeks of school, everyone seemed a little stir-crazy.

Heinous, playing samurai, jumped in front of a couple on their way to make out by the pond. "So-san, master of the poison tongue, meet your doom!" he said, moving his lips more than he actually spoke, like a poorly dubbed kung-fu movie.

The couple, a pair of PDA-happy Chess Club geeks, was struck speechless. They edged around Heinous and sped up.

"Your cowardice reflects on your ancestors!" Heinous called. "Many dragons will haunt you!"

Dickie and I headed across the square toward Sunny, who was sitting with Sage and Katy on a bench near the girls' dorm.

"Put a cream puff up your butt," Heinous sang, catching up to us. His most recent shtick involved making up lyrics to Eddie Murphy's classic, "Boogie in Your Butt."

"Put numchucks up your butt. Put a fluffy duck up your butt. Put an Oompa-Loompa up your butt."

"The humor in this particular saying," Dickie replied, mocking the way Mr. Funt, the sophomore class English teacher, spoke, "being that, technically speaking, an Oompa-Loompa would not fit up one's buttocks, not to mention the fact that Willy Wonka would never permit such egregious treatment of his workers. Thus, the ridiculousness of the claim, which leads to laughter."

"Put Sunny up your butt," Heinous said.

"The line, sir, has been crossed."

"Do you bite your thumb at me, sir?" Heinous asked, imitating one of the characters in a movie of *Romeo and Juliet* that Mr. Funt had made us watch.

"Aye, I bite my thumb."

"But do you bite your thumb at me?"

Dickie let the gag drop as we approached the bench

where the girls had gathered. The orange glow of street lamps illuminated the sidewalk. "Such a pleasure to find you out this evening," Dickie said, tipping his hat.

"The pleasure's all mine, sir," Sunny replied. She was good at playing along.

I said "Hi" to Sage, and she said "Nice hair" to me. After that I didn't know what to say, so I looked around. Sage and Katy went back to their previous conversation. They giggled and whispered to each other while Dickie and Sunny talked and Heinous threw in a few well-timed jokes.

My eyes drifted over the lamp-lit campus. It seemed like everyone, even the spotted mathletes, had found someone. I studied a few sophomore girls gathered by a concrete slab at the far end of the square. Sarah Parrot, Amber Lane, Jewel Sens, Brandy Morales—all of them were going out with someone. In their center, beside Mark Watson, the golden-crested senior thug, sat the Ice Queen. Mark was talking with some of his friends while Ellie was talking with the sophomore girls. The two of them together were a Hollywood picture of perfection.

I wondered what was wrong with me. Despite my recent rise in popularity, I still felt separated from everyone. It was as if I were staring through a window at all the real people talking and holding hands and laughing on the other side.

A water balloon smashed on the sidewalk near my leg.

"Blast!" Dickie said. "Looks like we might expect a bit of rain."

"Quite," I replied, straining for a British accent.

"Rather," Heinous said.

Two figures popped up from behind some bushes at the edge of the square and launched more balloons at us. One exploded on Sunny. She laughed, ever a good sport.

I recognized our attackers from the way they grunted while giving each other a high five. The Steves, aka Steve Lacone and Steve Dennon—two jeekish sophomores from Boomer wing.

"For your honor!" Dickie said, filling his hand with a snowball-size glop of shaving cream. He launched it at the Steves, but it disintegrated in midair.

"For freedom!" Heinous cried. He ran over the hill, spraying people with shaving cream. The Steves had a whole crew from Boomer wing who chucked water balloons at him.

I joined the fray along with Cheese and a few other Dingo-wingers who came to our aid until we had an all-out battle involving buckets of water from the pond. T-shirts were drenched and hair frothed with shaving cream. The RC on duty halfheartedly tried to get us to settle down, but there was no rule against water and shaving cream fights. Someone even managed to land a glop of cream on the RC's crotch, at which point he gave up and went inside.

Dickie and I chased Steve Lacone with a bucket full of pond water that we intended to dump on his head. As we rounded a corner, I slipped and skidded into a puddle.

Mud splattered from my feet to my cheek. It wouldn't have been bad, except two girls were standing right there.

One of the girls, with dark hair, silver eyebrow piercings, and a sly smile, stepped toward me while I sat there, dumb as a wet bunny in the lamplight. She wore a tight shirt cut low enough to reveal the black lines of Japanese characters tattooed on her chest, descending into her cleavage. I tried to keep myself from staring as she raised her hand and wiped a glop of mud off my shoulder. Then she touched my forehead with her muddy finger, dragging a line down the center of my nose.

"Cute," she said, and walked away.

Ultimate Freak

AS SOON AS I GOT BACK to my dorm, I looked through past yearbooks. It turned out that the girl who'd touched me was Jessica Keen, an incredibly hot junior from Chicago. For days following the water fight, I had this nervous, giddy energy. Except nothing happened. I kept an eye out for Jessica, but she hung with an entirely different crowd. The only time I saw her was when I went to the cafeteria. She sat at a corner table with Rachel Chang and some Goth guys, and she never looked my way.

I began to worry that she might be losing interest in me, if she ever had been interested. Maybe I'd only blipped onto her radar for a moment and now I'd been forgotten. My stomach twisted at the thought that history might keep repeating itself and I'd forever be overlooked.

Clearly, I had to do something. This new me couldn't let Jessica Keen get away.

It was Dickie who came up with an idea. Originally, he pitched Operation Ultimate Freak to Heinous and me as a way to protest the dismal cafeteria food. "Chicks love rebels with a cause," he said.

The tricky thing about the food service at ASMA was that at the beginning of the week it never seemed that bad. For instance, the pancakes that were served on Monday started off as a tasty breakfast treat. But on Wednesday the leftover pancakes reappeared for lunch as two pieces of bread with ham and cheese in between, forming round grilled sandwiches the menu dubbed "wagon wheels," and then, with the help of processed cheese and refried beans (that had also been used earlier that week), the "pancake enchilada" was born.

Mealtime outbursts in response to the food service's less edible choices were something of an ASMA tradition. In my short time there, I'd seen sword duels with stale churros, flying-tortilla battles, and chicken-patty hockey. All we planned was to take the classic notion of the food fight a step further.

"The oppressor always counts on the silence of the oppressed," Dickie said, trying to psych us up for what we were about to do.

I nodded, going along with him. I knew his justifications were completely bogus, but I didn't care. I didn't need any encouragement. Jessica Keen was reason enough for me.

To anyone sitting in the cafeteria that day, Operation Ultimate Freak probably looked something like this:

Trays are clattering and people are chatting, milling about between the round tables. Matt Reis, head of the Juggling Club, is working furiously to keep five stale buns aloft. On the table next to him, engineering geeks are building a tower out of forks, knives, and apples. Seniors are talking among themselves, stressed about test scores and colleges. A few upperclassmen flirt with sophomore girls at the popular table, while Ellie Frost acts uninterested and whispers to a friend. Nearby, Jessica sits at her corner table with Rachel Chang and some Goth guy. Altogether, it's the usual dinner scene.

Suddenly, a blond kid stands and throws his tray onto the floor. "That's it!" he yells. "I won't eat it anymore!"

People put down their silverware and stop tossing buns, wondering what this evening's entertainment will be. Blond Kid shouts at the top of his lungs, "NO . . . MORE . . . BEANS!" He clenches a fork in his fist like a killer in a horror movie. "DEATH TO THE PANCAKE ENCHILADA!" he cries as he runs across the cafeteria.

But who is he after?

Someone stands at the far end of the cafeteria—that quiet, brooding sophomore with the purple-and-orange punk hair. His fearless gaze meets the charging blond kid's. "You'll eat it and you'll like it," says Punk Guy, sounding vaguely like Clint Eastwood daring a criminal to make his day.

Whispers spread that they're roommates, which makes sense—bizarre explosions of rage among roommates are fairly common, yet Punk Guy seems composed. At the last second, he picks up a tray and, with a mighty baseball swing, smashes it against Blond Kid's face. A resounding thud echoes through the cafeteria as tray meets flesh. (Actually, I smacked Dickie's raised arm, but from where most people were sitting, they couldn't see that.)

Blond Kid's head snaps back, and he crumples to the ground. A hush falls over the cafeteria. He struggles to his feet and spits four bloody teeth onto a nearby table (white stones and a blood capsule). A girl yelps when one of the teeth lands in her corn.

All eyes are on Blond Kid. He wipes the blood off his face and strides toward his roommate. The fork has fallen from his hand, but he doesn't need a weapon. A circle of onlookers forms around them. Blond Kid shouts, "No more beans!"

The crowd picks up the chant, thumping their trays against the tables. "NO . . . MORE . . . BEANS! NO . . . MORE . . . BEANS!" thunders throughout the cafeteria.

The two sophomores square off. No longer are they mere roommates fighting. The chant transforms them into symbolic heroes of the daily cafeteria struggle—to eat or not to eat. They come together and lock arms. With a mighty twist, Blond Kid rips off Punk Guy's hand.

Punk Guy falls to his knees, gaping at the stump where his hand once was. Ragged tendons (spaghetti and sauce) drip from the wound while Blond Kid raises the severed hand in victory.

But wait—Punk Guy isn't done. With his good hand, he pulls a knife from his inside pocket. Blood squirts as he jabs the blade into his gloating roommate's back. Blond Kid gives a tremendous cry, then collapses, gurgling, to the floor. One-handed Punk Guy is not to be trifled with!

"Nooooo . . . !" yells someone from the far end of the cafeteria. Heads turn. That dark-haired obnoxious sophomore is standing on a cafeteria table. He pulls an old Western six-shooter from his pocket, aims it at Punk Guy, and fires.

Punk Guy stumbles back, grabbing his chest. Spots of blood darken his T-shirt. Obnoxious Guy fires four more shots. Punk Guy lurches with each one. At last he collapses, succumbing beside Jessica Keen's chair.

The smell of caps permeates the room, and the rest is silence.

I kept my eyes closed and tried to still my breathing to keep from laughing. It was perfect. With each shot, I'd imagined the pain searing through me. The ketchup packets taped to my chest were warm and sticky. Nothing had ever made me feel so alive as playing dead.

A few kids clapped, and more joined in until the cafeteria literally shook with applause. I opened my eyes a crack. Crowds had gathered around Dickie and me, then Jessica gave me a hand up. I got to my feet, and she leaned so close I thought she might kiss me.

"Nice one," she whispered, "for a soph."

Hassert, the RC on duty, barged through the crowd, sending students to their seats. "Get over here," he growled to Dickie and me. He already had Heinous by his shirt collar.

"See you later," Jessica said.

Hassert clamped his meaty hand onto my shoulder. He led us out, ranting about how we'd crossed the line and were going to face severe disciplinary action.

I didn't pay attention to any of it. All I could think about was Jessica Keen's warm breath tickling my cheek.

I **M**

HASSERT KEPT US IN his office for almost an hour, but Principal Durn, the man in charge of student discipline, was away at a conference, so he eventually had to let us go. "You'll be hearing from me soon," Hassert threatened. "This isn't over."

For the rest of the night, upperclassmen I'd never spoken to before called my name and slapped my back, while guys from Dingo wing acted out scenes from our performance, redoing parts in slow motion. The few who hadn't been in the cafeteria kept saying to me, "Man, I can't believe I missed it," as if they'd somehow let me down. People looked at me now like they had no doubt that the stories they'd heard were true. My image had been sealed.

After social hour, an instant message blipped onto my screen while I was working on a paper. Outside of checking my calculus answers with a couple other students in my class, I wasn't much into IMing people, and no one ever IM'd me.

I clicked "accept."

ghost44: Hello, James Turner.

johnnyrotten: Who is this?

ghost44: I'm a ghost. Are you a ghost too?

johnnyrotten: Not that I know of.

ghost44: I think you are. I think I recognize you.

johnnyrotten: From where?

ghost44: Where is a place, and the answer to that is rather obvious, since we're both here. The real question is why. Why would I recognize you?

johnnyrotten: Umm . . . because you've seen me before?

ghost44: Only in myself. I've seen you in myself. It takes a ghost to recognize a ghost.

johnnyrotten: Why am I a ghost?

ghost44: That's what happens when you die.

johnnyrotten: If you're talking about the cafeteria thing, you must not have heard—they saved me at the hospital. Pumped a few pints of ketchup into my veins and now I'm good as new.

ghost44: I doubt that. Not even ketchup, the miracle vegetable, could save you, dear James. Sometimes ghosts don't know that they're ghosts and then it's hopeless. But I knew you were one. I guessed it the first time I saw you. Today only made it clearer.

johnnyrotten: Because I pretended to die?

ghost44: The opposite, actually.

johnnyrotten: Now you've lost me.

ghost44: Ghosts pretend to be alive, and we're good at pretending—so good that we might even fool ourselves. You're lucky I found you.

johnnyrotten: Why's that?

ghost44: Because it's lonely being a ghost. Maybe I'll see you again. Will you see me?

johnnyrotten: That depends. What do you look like?

ghost44: A wisp of smoke.

ghost44: A reflection of light off the surface of a pond.

ghost44: A color seen out of the corner of your eye.

ghost44: But if you look straight at me, I'm one-hundred-percent invisible.

johnnyrotten: Who is this?

The ghost logged out.

Phone Call

I SPENT THE NEXT DAY trying to figure out who ghost44 might be. Jessica Keen was at the top of my list, but that seemed too good to be true. Girls like Jessica had never even looked at me before, not to mention writing me secret IMs. It could have been Sunny—that would explain why she had to keep things a secret, since she was going out with Dickie. Or it might be Sage Fisher. Sage was pretty cute in a busty, back-to-nature way, but I couldn't figure out why she'd call herself invisible.

When I got back to my dorm room after class, there were two letters slipped under my door. At first I thought they might be from ghost44, but my excitement soon derailed when I saw the official-looking ASMA stationery. One letter was addressed to me, and the other to Dickie.

Beneath the NOTICE OF A DISCIPLINARY HEARING heading it said, "Regrettably, the hearing will have to be delayed until after the weekend, due to scheduling." Only Hassert would start a sentence like that with "Regrettably." From day one, he'd had it in for me. He had his favorites, and he had the students he despised, and he made no bones about it. "I don't like your attitude," he'd say. Or, "I know what you're up to" (which always made me chuckle, since *I* never knew what I was up to).

A tight knot of dread lodged in my chest when I read the paragraph in the letter that said our parents would be notified. Dickie read his letter at the same time as me, then tacked it to the wall over his desk.

"My first act of civil disobedience," he said, as if the letter was something to be proud of. He promptly called his parents to explain how ridiculous the charges against him were, given that no one had gotten hurt and no rules were broken. According to Dickie, his most recent "performance art event" had been a resounding success.

I realized, listening to his enthusiastic conversation with his parents, that I wasn't worried about my parents being angry with me. What bothered me was having to deal with my parents at all. I wanted to keep my life at ASMA completely separate, but if the school called them, my parents might show up for the hearing on Monday.

I pictured my dad thumping the walls of the main building while Moms fussed over my purple hair and chatted with people about how I used to fear cats. Anyone who met my parents would know I wasn't the person I claimed to be. They were the kryptonite to my Superman. Without even trying, they'd ruin everything.

Our phone rang several times that afternoon, but I didn't answer it. I couldn't even listen to my mom's voice on the machine without feeling ill. Unfortunately, Dickie picked up the phone later before I could stop him. "Certainly, Mrs. Turner, he's right here," he said, handing the phone to me. *Good luck,* he mouthed.

The knot of dread rose to my throat. I took the phone and carried it into the bathroom for privacy.

"Hey," I said.

"Jaaames," Moms replied. "Where've you been? We've been calling all day. Didn't you get our messages? We left a dozen or so on your machine, and then it stopped working."

She was off and running, laying on the worried-parent act. In truth, there were only two messages on the machine before I unplugged it, but she loved to exaggerate.

"Are you there, James?"

When I spoke, it was in a dull, flat voice. "I'm right here."

"Then why didn't you call us back?" Moms asked. "Don't you check your machine? I think it must be broken."

"The machine's fine. I've been busy."

"Are they giving you too much work? It's not good to work too hard. You have to take breaks. At least it's

Friday and tomorrow you can come home. How does that sound? We'll pick you up tomorrow morning, then we can go clothes shopping. Wouldn't that be fun?"

"I hate shopping."

"I think you need sweaters," Moms continued. "It'll be cold soon."

"I don't need sweaters."

"Honey, you can't go around wearing ripped-up clothes. You look like a bum. Tomorrow morning we'll pick you up and get you something nice. And then we can chat."

"Chat?"

"About things . . ."

"What things?" I asked, playing dumb.

That stumped her. The phone crackled, then my dad cleared his throat. He must have been on the bedroom phone listening in. My parents always did that—they'd both be on the line, but only Moms would talk. I could picture her pinching the cordless between her head and shoulder, giving my dad a frustrated look while mouthing *Say something.*

"James, we got a phone call," Dad grumbled, breaking his customary silence. "Mr. Hassert explained that you were involved in a disturbing incident."

"It wasn't disturbing."

"Then why did they call us?" pounced Moms, like a professional wrestler tagging in. "I mean really?"

"It's no big deal," I said. "Hassert just doesn't have a sense of humor."

"And now there's this hearing. We should be there."

"No. Definitely not."

"But they called us," she repeated.

I scrambled to change the subject. "Look, about this weekend, I've got a lot of work to do. There's a chemistry study group and I need to get notes."

"Wouldn't you rather come home?"

"I can't."

Moms paused. "What's wrong with you?"

"Nothing's wrong."

"You don't sound right to me."

"What am I supposed to say to that?" I asked. "I mean, really, do I sound 'right' now?"

"No. You don't." She addressed my dad: "Does he sound right to you?"

"How about this, Mother? Is this better? It's lovely weather out."

"Honestly, you don't sound like yourself," she said.

"Too bad. This is me."

"Okay, okay," Moms replied. "So when should we pick you up? Tomorrow night? That doesn't make much sense. If you come home tomorrow night and leave Sunday afternoon, that's hardly worth the drive."

"I can't miss this study session," I lied.

"You want us to drive all the way out there and pick you up tomorrow night?"

"No. I have to write a paper on Sunday."

"But . . ."

"I can't help it," I said. "I have a ton of work to do. Lots of kids aren't going home."

Moms fell silent. After a few seconds, Dad chimed in, giving it one more shot. "What your mom's trying to say is that we'd like to see you this weekend."

"That's right," Moms exclaimed. "We want you to be with us."

"I know. I just can't go home right now."

"You're acting very strange," Moms said, but the wind had gone out of her sails.

"I have to go."

"I think they work you too hard. You need to take breaks."

"Bye."

"James . . ."

I hung up before she could say "wait" or "I love you" or any of that stuff. A low buzzing filled my head. I should have felt guilty for being such a lousy son, yet I didn't feel anything.

Some guys laughed in the hallway outside my door. Since it was a Friday, we didn't have to be in our rooms until midnight. Normally, I would have headed out to join them, but I wasn't in the mood to deal with people anymore. Instead, I went to sleep.

Dream Guides

"SIT ANYWHERE, HONEY," *said a waitress in a powder-blue dress.*

I was in a diner. The comforting smell of coffee filled the air while voices murmured and silverware clanked. The place seemed crowded, but every table had an open seat, as if they were all waiting for someone to arrive.

The waitress walked away, leaving me to choose a spot on my own.

I wove between the tables toward the back. A man in a black coat hunched in the corner, playing with a lighter. The woman sitting next to him rubbed a butter knife against her shirt and checked her teeth in the reflection. I paused before their booth.

"Well?" the man grumbled. "We won't bite."

"Speak for yourself," the woman said.

I slid into the booth seat across from them, and the woman handed me a cup of coffee. "Three sugars, no cream."

"How'd you know?"

"Wild guess."

She introduced herself as Kiana and the man as Nick. I started to reply, but Nick cut me off. "We know who you are," he said. "The question is, J.T., do you?"

"What do you mean?"

Neither one of them answered. I took a sip of my coffee. It was cold and a little too sweet.

"Drink up," Nick said, standing. "There's something we need to show you."

I took another sip before following them out through a back door into the alley. A nearby Dumpster overflowed with garbage, tainting the air with the smell of rotting fruit and coffee grounds. Kiana shut the door behind me. She leaned against the brick wall, crossing her arms.

Nick drew a long samurai sword from beneath his coat. The blade flashed silver as he raised it before him. "You think you're a tough guy, don't you? A real fighter?"

I glared at him, not saying anything.

"If you're a fighter, then this belongs to you." He held out the sword, offering it to me. "Take it."

I reached for the hilt. Before I could grab it, Nick snapped his wrist, slashing the blade across my arm.

The pain shocked me. I clenched my wrist. "I'm dreaming," I said, surprised by how much it hurt.

"Tell that to the judge," Nick replied. He offered the sword to me again.

I looked at Kiana. "Go on, J.T.," she said. "Prove that it's yours. If you master the pain, you master yourself."

I reached for it again, but Nick gave me another slash on the arm.

"Just a dream, right, bud?" He rested the blade against his shoulder.

I tried one last time to take the sword. Nick only had to move the slightest bit before I flinched.

He shook his head, giving me the same dismissive look that people always had. "We're wasting our time on this one," he said. "He's nothing special."

Blueberry Tarts

I STAYED IN BED the next morning, not wanting to sleep anymore and not wanting to get up. The dream had felt so real that I kept checking my arm for cuts. After lying awake awhile, hunger finally got the better of me. I hurried out to snag breakfast before the cafeteria closed.

Campus appeared eerily empty. Most students who lived within a few hours of ASMA had probably gone home for the weekend. Even Dickie had left, dragging a sack of dirty laundry out early that morning.

I ran into Sage on my way into the main building. "James!" she called. "Are you going to be here tomorrow?"

"Sure."

Sage seemed so happy she could barely contain herself. "My dad's coming to visit!" she said. "It's his weekend to see me, and he wants to have a picnic. Will you come?"

"To the picnic?"

"He wants to meet my friends. You'll like him."

"I don't know," I teased, thinking of the IM I'd gotten from ghost44. Was this what she meant by seeing me again? "Tomorrow is Tater Tot casserole day. I'd hate to miss those crispy, golden Tater Tots, dripping in creamy sauce with mushy carrots and gray peas."

She smiled. "I'll take that as a yes."

Sunday turned out to be a beautiful, blue-sky day. Sage's dad burst into her dorm around one, bearing a large wicker picnic basket and a smile that crinkled his eyes. I'd seen him once before, on the day all the parents had helped their kids move in. He was older than most parents, but he didn't act old. He looked like how I imagined Socrates would have—tan skin, a wild nest of white hair, scruffy face, and round belly—except instead of a toga, he wore faded blue jeans and a button-down shirt, open at the top.

He dropped the basket as soon as he entered and gave Sage a hug, swinging her off her feet. I looked away, but neither Sage nor her dad seemed to care. Afterward, Sage introduced me. Her dad clamped my hand in both of his and studied my face. "Ah, yes," he said. "Sage has told me about you."

I wanted to ask what she'd said, but Mr. Fisher had already moved on. "Who's hungry?" he asked in a loud voice.

A few students watching TV or doing homework in the commons glanced up, perplexed.

"I brought plenty of food," Mr. Fisher announced, raising the wicker basket. "Enough lunch for everyone."

He took Sage by the hand and headed for the door. Several students hung back, wondering if the invitation applied to them. "Come on," he called to the stragglers. "It's too beautiful to stay inside."

Mr. Fisher led us behind the dorms to the far side of the pond, stopping at a spot we called the cleavage since it lay between two small hills. He spread a blanket on the grass and gestured for everyone to sit.

Sage sat next to her dad, practically glowing. The rest of the kids were an odd mix of Sage's friends and students who'd happened to be in the commons when Mr. Fisher had announced his promise of free food. Donald Smails, the chess master, came, along with Muppet, Tracy Lang, Katy Cameron, and the Ice Queen.

Lately, pretending that Ellie didn't exist had gotten to be more difficult. For the last week, all anyone talked about was how Mark Watson and her had split up. According to reports, Mark had been expelled for running across campus, swimming the pond, and punching out some guy simply because he was walking with Ellie. The incident had made Ellie a bit of a legend. Senior class officers even started taking orders for T-shirts commemorating the "Mark Watson Run, Swim, and Box for Ellie Triathlon." Everyone wanted one.

I'd learned to handle being in physics class with Ellie, but sitting next to her at a picnic made me nervous in an entirely new way. I kept worrying that my stomach might rumble or I'd sneeze or do something dumb. I couldn't even figure out how to sit. After fidgeting for a few minutes, I tried crossing my legs, but I bumped Ellie's knee.

"Sorry," I mumbled.

Ellie didn't say anything. Fortunately, Mr. Fisher filled the silence. He pulled things out of the picnic basket like a magician conjuring objects from a hat.

"Beaujolais Nouveau," he said, lifting a large bottle of wine from the basket. "And Dixie cups."

"Uh, Mr. Fisher," Muppet squeaked, "isn't that against ASMA policy?"

"Call me Liam," he replied while opening the bottle. He filled the Dixie cups and passed them around. "What's bread and cheese without a little wine?"

Next Liam pulled food out of the baskets. "French bread!" he announced, holding up two halves of a baguette. He smelled the bread, then handed it to Sage. She tore off a hunk and passed it on, smiling at me.

"Brie!" Liam said, holding up a wheel of cheese. He passed the cheese around with his pocketknife. Everyone cut off a sliver. I ate the cheese and some bread. The rich, buttery flavor blended well with the wine. "Camembert!" he said, holding up another wheel of cheese once everyone had finished the Brie. Then, "Chèvre!" which tasted delicious.

After the cheeses, Liam pulled out a single nectarine and cut it into slices. "Food of the gods," he said, raising his bushy white eyebrows.

We all took a slice. It was the sweetest, most perfectly ripened nectarine I'd ever tasted. Juice dribbled down my chin. I wiped my face with my sleeve, hoping the Ice Queen hadn't seen.

Then came mango and pear. Grapes. Gouda. Swiss cheese. Cucumber slices. Prosciutto. Melon. Orange slices. Oregon cherries. Zucchini bread. Liam named each item before passing it around.

I watched Ellie take tiny, delicate bites of things, chewing slowly and leaving perfectly arranged uneaten remains on her napkin. Compared to how she ate, I was an ogre. I tried to focus on savoring each bite like she did, but she must have noticed me looking at her. She glanced at me, then folded up her napkin and hid it away.

Between rounds, Liam filled our Dixie cups and told us stories.

"You know what Inuit children eat in the fall?" he said, tearing off a hunk of French bread. Crumbs sprinkled his belly. "In the fall, the arctic ptarmigan feeds almost exclusively on blueberries. It's a very well-camouflaged bird, and its instinct is to freeze when a predator approaches. So if the children spot a bird, they grab it and snap its neck." Liam made a motion with his hands, as if opening a bottle. "Then they cut out the bird's stomach, which is packed with blueberries, roast it over a fire, and eat it like a blueberry tart."

He told other stories about the Arctic, too. Sage had mentioned that her dad was a geologist, and I guess he traveled to some remote places. In one story, he talked about a starving polar bear that lumbered into his camp. "At first I thought the bear might eat our dog," he said. "Until I noticed the dog's tail wagging. For hours, the two of them played like old friends, before the bear lumbered off." He looked around the circle, eyeing us. "Loneliness," he said, "is worse than hunger."

After we finished the food, Liam rummaged around his basket again. "Dessert," he said, pulling out three large strawberries.

He held each strawberry in the waning sunlight and studied them carefully. Finally, he selected one, took a small bite, and passed it on. We each took a tiny bite. None of us spoke as the strawberries were passed. Perhaps it was the wine. Normally, I never would have shared a strawberry with Donald Smails or Muppet, but at the time the whole thing seemed perfectly natural.

The first strawberry tasted tangy and sharp, the second swelled with sweetness, and the third looked like a deep red heart with golden stars speckling the skin. I watched the Ice Queen take a bite. When she passed the strawberry to me, I bit in the same place she had, tasting the half-moon left by her teeth.

Liam placed his hands on his knees and surveyed the campus. "This is a good place," he said.

I nodded. In that moment, I felt like all was right with the world.

Most students returned to campus later that evening. People filtered back to their normal groups, as if the picnic had never happened. Sage giggled with the drama girls, Muppet huddled with the gamer geeks, and Ellie was probably off holding court with the Barbie wannabes. All the usual social barriers were back in place.

I wandered away from the square and thought about some of the things that Liam had said. He'd talked about fish who changed gender when they reached a certain age and an island in the tropics where a percentage of the populace didn't become male or female until their late teens. "Of course, we're all part man and part woman," he'd said. According to Liam, we all had a missing half somewhere—a person who was us but not us, and if only we found them, we'd be whole. Maybe he was full of crap, but the way Liam talked made me yearn to find my missing half. Except it couldn't be that easy. There must have been something messing it up and keeping people apart, because I'd never known anyone who wasn't still searching for something.

When I got to the far end of campus, I saw Ellie sitting on a bench outside her dorm. I thought of how my lips had touched the strawberry where hers had been. In a way, she seemed lonely like me. I imagined saying hello, and her smiling and laughing as we fell into a deep, witty conversation. After all, if polar bears and dogs could play together and fish could change gender, why not this?

"Hey," I said, strolling up to the bench where she sat.

Ellie gave me a surprised, wary look.

"That was weird, wasn't it?" I asked.

"What was?"

"The picnic today."

Her eyes narrowed. "I liked it. I didn't think it was weird at all."

I shrugged, afraid that I was blowing my chance. "I'm James, by the way—the roommate slayer. You know, from the cafeteria thing."

"I know." Ellie looked away. "I wasn't impressed."

Before I could say anything else, Amber Lane came out of the dorm behind us. "Ellie!" she called. "I've been searching everywhere for you. There's free pizza in the boys' dorm."

Ellie smiled at Amber with something close to relief.

"*Everyone's* over there," Amber said, taking Ellie's hand. "We have to go."

"Sure," Ellie replied. She gave me a sidelong glance as she left. "See you later."

I wanted to kick myself for thinking that she'd ever want to talk to me.

Bumper Stickers

ghost44: "I'm nobody! Who are you? Are you nobody too?"

johnnyrotten: Apparently. Why do you ask?

ghost44: It's from an Emily Dickinson poem.

johnnyrotten: I don't know it.

ghost44: Did you know she spent a large part of her life secluded in her house, talking to guests through a door?

johnnyrotten: That's creepy.

ghost44: I don't think so. I think it's beautiful. She lived through her words.

johnnyrotten: Did she have cats?

ghost44: I believe she was a dog person.

johnnyrotten: Poor dog. Do you have cats?

ghost44: No. I tried having a goldfish once, but it jumped out a window and killed itself.

johnnyrotten: No kidding?

ghost44: No kidding. It was sitting in a bowl near my bedroom window, and it launched itself out one day. I found it on the sidewalk, baking in the sun.

johnnyrotten: Ick.

ghost44: I know. It didn't even leave a note.

johnnyrotten: How selfish.

ghost44: Anyway, I'm not like Emily Dickinson, if that's what you're wondering. I couldn't live my life secluded in a house. I'm just saying, I can understand why she did it.

johnnyrotten: So what are you like?

ghost44: Hmmm . . . The main thing about me is I'm shy.

johnnyrotten: You don't seem shy.

ghost44: That's because there are many types of shy. There's the type where someone can't talk with people, and this other type, where you might talk all the time, but you can't say what matters. Except to you. I can confess things to you.

johnnyrotten: Because I'm a ghost too?

ghost44: Bravo! I knew you'd catch on.

johnnyrotten: Did I see you this weekend?

ghost44: That depends. Can you see ghosts?

johnnyrotten: Maybe.

ghost44: Your turn. I told you something about myself. Now tell me something.

johnnyrotten: Like what? Like I secretly fantasize about sheep in tutus?

ghost44: Tell me something real. What's your bumper sticker?

johnnyrotten: I don't have a car.

ghost44: It's not that type of bumper sticker. Didn't you read *Ordinary People?*

johnnyrotten: I think that book was banned at my old school.

ghost44: Tragic. You'd expect they'd get a little more up-to-date with their book bannings. Anyhow, a bumper sticker is a quote that defines you. Something that explains the way you look at the world.

johnnyrotten: Uh . . . how about "Hang in There!"

ghost44: Really?

johnnyrotten: Yeah. I'm a big fan of that poster with the little kitten dangling off a branch.

ghost44: Ha, ha. Seriously, what quote would you choose?

johnnyrotten: Give me a minute.

johnnyrotten: How about this: "I am certain of nothing but the holiness of the heart's affections and the truth of imagination— what the imagination seizes as beauty must be truth—whether it existed before or not."

ghost44: That's a long bumper sticker.

johnnyrotten: It's Keats. I'm reading him for English—thought I'd try to impress you.

ghost44: Well, not to offend any dead white males out there, but I have to disagree with Keats. As far as I can tell, beauty and truth don't have anything to do with each other. They seem more the opposite to me.

johnnyrotten: How so?

ghost44: Beauty is deceptive. It's an illusion. It distracts us from the truth. The poet Valéry defined beauty as the thing that leads to desperation.

johnnyrotten: Are you a teacher?

ghost44: God, no, you sicko. I just read a lot.

johnnyrotten: Why won't you tell me who you are?

ghost44: That would take all the fun away.

johnnyrotten: At least give me a hint.

ghost44: I already have.

johnnyrotten: ?

ghost44: Anyhow, I wanted to wish you good luck at your disciplinary hearing. I hope you don't get kicked out tomorrow.

johnnyrotten: Would you miss me if I was?

ghost44: Of course. I need someone to haunt.

Look-Alike Weapons

ON MONDAY, DICKIE, HEINOUS, and I were pulled from our normal classes, which was the one perk of having a disciplinary hearing. All the students in my chemistry lab grew quiet when Ms. Pritchett, the secretary, called me to the office over the PA system. I smirked and stuffed my hands into my pockets as I left to hide the fact that I was trembling.

On the way to the office, Dickie, Heinous, and I joked with each other. Dickie, who planned on being a lawyer, felt certain we couldn't get suspended. He'd read through the entire student handbook. Although fighting was listed as a suspendable offense, there was nothing prohibiting play fighting. "We were merely exercising our freedom of expression," he said. "Call it performance art."

"Right-o," I quipped, doing my best to sound nonchalant—like getting in trouble was old hat for me. "We're actors!"

"It's not our fault if they don't have a sense of humor," Heinous said.

"If they can't appreciate art," Dickie said.

"Blast!" I added. "We should have sold tickets."

Ms. Pritchett led us into a conference room and gave us each a yellow legal pad and a pen. She seated us apart from each other and told us to write down our versions of what had happened.

Heinous finished his in no time and began adding diagrams of the performance, which he flashed to us across the room. He labeled one of the drawings "The Single Bullet Theory." It was a detailed illustration of the possible trajectory of one imaginary bullet that somehow hit a stick figure version of me six times. I was so nervous, even the stupidest things made me laugh. Ms. Pritchett stuck her head into the room and scolded me for talking.

Dickie approached his written account more seriously. He kept chewing his pen and flipping through the student handbook he'd brought with him, as if composing a legal brief. It took him at least twenty minutes before he finished.

When we were done, Ms. Pritchett collected our legal pads and led us into Principal Durn's office. Doughy-faced Hassert sat off to the side with his hands folded on his lap like a maniacal supervillain. All he needed was a fluffy white cat to stroke and the image would have been complete. Clearly, he'd already told Principal Durn his version of events.

Ms. Pritchett gave Principal Durn the legal pads and seated us in three chairs arranged before his desk. Principal Durn, a small black man with a deep voice and dark circles under his eyes, flipped through our statements. His bald head, ringed by a nimbus of peppery hair, made him resemble a monk. I liked him—he didn't pretend to be a big shot like other principals I'd known, and he always spoke politely, treating students as adults.

"Richard Lang," he said to Dickie, "it says here that you, quote, 'fail to see how performance art without malicious intent could be construed as fighting with the intent of injury.'"

"Yes, sir," Dickie replied.

Principal Durn nodded and continued to read. "'The performance was merely a commentary on the inherent violence of eating at a cafeteria which condones the consumption of animals, while concealing the inhumane reality of their treatment.'"

Dickie nodded. "I'm particularly concerned about the chicken-fried steak."

Out of the corner of my eye, I saw Heinous's shoulders shake as he tried to keep from laughing. I clenched my jaw to appear like I was stifling laughter, too, but the truth was I couldn't stop thinking about what would happen if I got kicked out of ASMA. I'd die if I had to go back to my old school.

Principal Durn moved on to the next legal pad. "James Turner," he said, looking at me.

"Yes, sir?" My face froze in a fake grin.

"According to your account, Mr. Lang charged at you with a fork in his fist. You pretended to slap Mr. Lang with a tray. Then you proceeded to scuffle with him until your, quote, 'limb was removed'?"

"That's right," I said, barely able to force out enough breath to speak.

Principal Durn continued, "If I understand things correctly, you stabbed Mr. Lang in the back with a stage knife and pretended to be shot to death while activating numerous blood packets on your chest? As you wrote, 'tomato spurts regaled the crowd.'"

"It was ketchup," I explained.

"Mr. Turner?"

"Nothing."

Principal Durn turned to Heinous. "Henry Chavez, you state, 'I went Bang! Bang! and J.T. went down. I capped him. Victory was mine. The forces of evil were avenged.'"

"You see," Heinous said in his I'm-just-trying-to-be-helpful voice, "'capped' is a pun."

"I see." Principal Durn continued to read off the pad. "'The bloodfest was meant to reveal the hypocrisy of a patriarchal culture which applauds the presentation of violence in the media, but not the exposure of breasts.'"

"That's it exactly," Heinous said. "I think I'd be a better person had I been raised seeing less violence on TV and more breasts."

"You boys think you're so smart," interrupted Hassert, a scowl creasing his face. "Everything's a joke you can just talk your way out of. Never mind the mess you created. Never mind the destruction of state property or the disruption of school. Never mind the three security guards who were called in. Do you realize, *Henry,* that if we'd had an armed security guard on duty, you could have been shot? You didn't think about that, did you? How funny would that be?"

"It was a cap gun," Heinous replied, pointing to the confiscated weapon on Principal Durn's desk. "Kids use cap guns."

"Look-alike weapons are illegal," Hassert said.

"How many guns have you seen with orange plastic tips?"

"You ought to be expelled."

"With all due respect," Dickie said, "there's nothing in the handbook prohibiting cap guns."

"Not only a look-alike gun," Hassert continued. "You used a knife as well."

"It was a stage knife," I said, leaving off the part that I'd swiped it from the school's theater supplies.

"Well, *James,* that looks like a real knife to me. Don't you think it looks real, *James?*"

I hated the way Hassert said my name.

"Six-year-olds can buy cap guns," Heinous said. "When I was a kid, I had a cap gun."

Hassert's jowls shook. "Not here! Not in school!"

"Are look-alike hands illegal, too?" Dickie asked. "What about look-alike blood? Or look-alike teeth? Are you going to outlaw ketchup and fillings?"

Hassert shook his plump finger at us. "Ever since you three arrived, you've abused opportunities." His glare settled on me.

I was still grinning, mostly because I didn't know what else to do.

"Quit smirking, smart-ass!" snapped Hassert.

"That'll do," Principal Durn said. "Mr. Hassert, I'd like a word with these gentlemen. Alone."

"I'm keeping my eye on you," Hassert mumbled as he left. "All of you," he added, but his gaze stayed on me.

After Hassert left, Principal Durn took his glasses off and rubbed his eyes. He didn't say anything. For a long time, the only sound in his office was the ticking clock.

"Are we getting suspended?" Dickie asked.

"No."

"Can I have my cap gun back?" Heinous asked.

"No."

Principal Durn took a deep breath, scratched his cheek, and tugged his ear. He looked exhausted. Finally, he got up and pulled a yearbook off the shelf. The picture on the cover was of a different school.

"Did you know that before I came here, I was the principal at East Jefferson High?"

We shook our heads.

"Seven years. It was quite a change for me coming here," he said, sitting down and flipping through the yearbook. "There were good students at East Jefferson. They may not have been able to score as high on tests as students here can, but they were smart. And they didn't have one-tenth the opportunities you three do."

Here it comes, I thought, the speech about how privileged we were to get this great education from the state.

"Look." Principal Durn pointed to a picture in the yearbook of a kid with a broad forehead and a huge smile. "John Sandia," he said. "Triple varsity. Football, basketball, and baseball. He kept a scrapbook of every game he played in. The thing is, he didn't write about his own accomplishments in that scrapbook. He wrote about what the players on the other teams had done. What great athletes the others were."

Principal Durn tapped on the page next to John's picture, then he flipped back a few pages and indicated a picture of a girl with curly dark hair, glasses, and a few blemishes on her cheeks. "That's Lynn Frillo," he said. "The most gifted poet I've ever met. She wrote lines that gave me chills. And then there's Robert Stone." He pointed to a student on the opposite page with a strong jaw and muscular neck. "Robert had two younger sisters he walked to school every day. He made them lunch every day. He picked them up after school every day. And he helped them with their homework *every day.*"

Principal Durn let us study the pictures of these other students we'd never met. "Do you know what they had in common?" he asked.

"They worked hard?" Heinous offered.

"Yes. They did," Principal Durn said. He turned the book toward himself and looked at the pictures again. "They worked hard, and each of them was shot and killed while I was principal at East Jefferson High."

I looked at the pictures again—those small, upside-down faces who'd lived and died for real.

"Now do you see why I fail to find your prank funny?" he asked.

"Yes, sir," Dickie replied.

Heinous nodded.

I stayed silent, staring at the pictures.

School had ended by the time Principal Durn dismissed us. We filed out and strolled the empty hallway. Once we left the main building, Heinous made a joke about how we should start a "less violence, more breasts" campaign, and Dickie offered to make the pamphlets.

I forced myself to joke with them, but my laughter sounded empty. I was a cardboard cutout of a person—a flat look-alike trying to pass myself off as real. I worried that Dickie and Heinous might hear the hollowness in my voice and know that I was all lies, paper thin.

We made our way to our dorm. Dickie turned on the commons TV and they crashed on the couch. I tried to hang out, only the phony feeling wouldn't go away. After a few minutes, I claimed that I needed to do homework and locked myself in my bathroom.

My hand brushed my purple and orange-streaked hair as I stared in the mirror. It felt like someone else's hand—as if I were stuck outside my body, floating two feet back. Disconnected. "This is me," I whispered, but my voice wasn't convincing.

I opened the medicine cabinet and took out the Swiss Army knife that my dad had given me. The blade flashed silver and sharp. I imagined fighting with it, like I'd claimed I'd done. Then I pressed the blade against the inside of my forearm until the cool edge dented my skin. If I was going to be someone, I had to commit myself. I had to earn it.

I jerked the blade across the pale skin of my forearm. Red welled into the gap, and with it came the pain—a hot, purifying burn that filled my body. I cut myself a few more times, thinking of the scars I'd have. Each would be proof for my stories. Evidence that I was someone who'd fought and struggled and had survived something real.

After rinsing the cuts, I wrapped them in my ketchup-stained T-shirt from the ultimate freak. Blood soaked into the fibers. The ketchup stains were a shallow orange-red, but real blood looked darker. When it dried, it was almost brown.

Cuts

"BACK AGAIN," NICK SAID.

They were sitting in the same corner booth of the diner. Nick was stacking plastic half-and-half containers into a pyramid. Kiana took the top one off and poured it into her coffee.

"That's mine," I said, nodding to the sword that lay across the table.

Nick grinned. "You sure about that?"

"Go easy on him, Nick," Kiana said. She swirled another cream into her coffee.

I held out my arm to show them the cuts. "It's mine," I repeated.

Nick stood and raised the sword. He slashed, only this time I didn't flinch. I didn't try to avoid the pain anymore. It was the price that had to be paid.

My hand rose to meet the blade, and the metal bit into my palm. A thrill coursed through me. Master the pain, master yourself.

I twisted the sword free of Nick's grasp. Then I flipped it around, pointing the blade at him. My bloody fingers settled into the worn leather grooves of the hilt.

"Well done!" Kiana said.

Nick shrugged. "It's a start."

Part II

The jaws of darkness do devour it up;
So quick bright things come to confusion.
— *A MIDSUMMER NIGHT'S DREAM*, ACT 1, SCENE 1

FaLL

GUSTS OF COOL AIR SHOT like adrenaline through my veins, laced with the leaf-burning, pumpkin-smashing, apple-fermenting scent of fall. Fall's my favorite season. I always feel more alive then, as if, on some primal level, my body knows it's my last chance to run wild before winter. I think everyone feels that a little. We're like stags bucking horns. I guess that's why football season's in the fall—the ancient autumnal need to bash heads. Except ASMA didn't field a football team. Soccer was our only fall sport.

I wasn't much into watching soccer, but sometimes I went to games to be outside and get rowdy with the crowd. ASMA usually lost in every sport except chess. Nonetheless, it was fun to taunt the opposing teams. Nothing like a stand full of geeks shouting, "That's all right. That's okay. You're gonna work for us someday," to piss off visiting jocks.

Our cheerleaders were especially talented. Since the administration had banned all "inappropriate" cheers, they took to making up cheers that no one except geeks would understand. Things like "FORGET DEFENSE. DE-FENESTRATE!" Or "KICK THEIR *G-L-U-T-E-U-S M-A-X-I-M-U-S.*" Then the cheerleaders would shout, "GLUTEUS!" And the crowd would shout, "MAXIMUS!"

Keep in mind, this is a school where the administration had chosen quarks as our mascot. Chants of "TAKE THEM TO THE ABATTOIR!" were as close as we could get to being rowdy without getting in trouble. We might not have been good at sports, but the fact that the opposing team needed a dictionary to figure out what we called them gave a certain satisfaction.

The day my old high school came to play our soccer team, I almost didn't go. I worried that someone from my hometown might recognize me, and I didn't want anyone from ASMA to find out about who I used to be. Besides, I liked that I'd vanished from my old school without an explanation. I pictured kids who'd once sat next to me in Algebra spending their days wondering where I'd gone. Maybe Kinsey Jackson regretted not giving me an *H.* Maybe she worried that I'd died or that she'd missed her chance with me and now I'd moved to someplace better.

Through the open window of my dorm room, I heard the crowd chanting, "*T-R-O-G-L-O-D-Y-T-E-S!* THAT'S

RIGHT. GO HOME, YOU TROGLODYTES!" and I felt a little proud. Since it was a Friday, everyone was at the game. Being the only guy left in my dorm started to depress me. I finally put on my coat, messed up my hair, and headed for the field.

The first half was nearly over by the time I reached the stands. Dickie and Heinous were in their usual seats, heckling the athletes. Sunny sat with Dickie, and Katy and Sage were on her other side. I spotted Ellie in the stands as well, sitting with the beautiful people, but I did my best to ignore her as I walked up the bleachers.

I sat next to Heinous. He kept standing and pulling up his shirt to expose his nipple every time the goalie looked over. "Yeah, baby," he said. "Watch it. You're under my nipple power. Oh, yeah. Can't stop looking over, can you?"

At halftime, people wandered around to get sodas and flirt. Dickie and Sunny were having a tickle war. Heinous bragged about how he should get a varsity letter, since his nipple had scored our only goal. I watched the players from my old high school eat orange slices while being lectured by their coach. I knew the names of almost everyone on their team.

At the start of the second half, Jessica Keen and Rachel Chang sat in front of us, so close that Jessica's back almost touched my knees. She looked wickedly cute in a black skirt, fishnet stockings, boots, and an old army coat. Dickie leaned over and gave me a sly grin. "She's into you," he whispered.

"Yeah, right," I whispered back. "She's a junior."

I tried to pretend that I wasn't interested, but my eyes kept drifting over to her. I imagined what it would feel like to brush my fingers along the slope of her neck down to the hem of her loose-collared shirt. Then I remembered the tattoo I'd glimpsed between her breasts, and I wondered what it said and what she thought of me and if she might be ghost44.

A few days earlier, I'd told Dickie and Heinous about the mysterious messages I'd received. They got a kick out of trying to guess who might be sending them. Heinous thought it was Frank Wood. "I bet it's a guy," he said. "That's why he wants to keep things secret."

After the game, Jessica turned and smiled at Dickie and me. "Hey, sophlings," she said. "What are you up to?"

I was too stunned to speak. Luckily, Dickie took over and invited everyone back to our wing to play a game. We filtered out of the stands and headed for our dorm, walking past the teams scattered on the sidelines, gathering their things.

"James!" someone shouted. I spotted George Kaplanski, a guy I'd known since kindergarten, staring at me. He raised his dark eyebrows. "James Turner?" he repeated, sounding less certain.

Jessica and Rachel were a few feet ahead. They didn't seem to have noticed George's calls. I paused. In all the years I'd gone to school with George Kaplanski, I don't think he'd ever once said my name. Part of me wanted to go back and talk with him, but if I did, I might lose my chance with Jessica.

I kept walking, hurrying to catch up to the others.

George didn't call my name again.

The girls had to get passes to come into our wing. Katy and Sage claimed they needed to go back to their dorm to pack since they were going home for the weekend, but Sunny, Rachel, and Jessica all signed in for half-hour passes. Mike, the RC on duty, eyed us suspiciously and reminded us to keep four feet on the floor and the door propped open at all times so he could make sure no one was breaking the rules. Whenever Mike patrolled the halls, he'd shout "No babies! No babies!" as he walked, which was his way of promoting the school's abstinence policy.

Jessica suggested playing hide-and-seek. I propped open the door to our room and Heinous did the same with his so we'd have more places to hide. Dickie volunteered to be It, probably so he could chase Sunny. The two of them had become an official "serious thing." Dickie even had notches on his bedpost from how many times they'd done it. I knew that's what the notches were for, although I'd never actually asked. Sex seemed only theoretically possible to me, the way walking on the moon or becoming president was possible.

I snuck off to my room and hid in my closet. Each room had two freestanding closets that could be locked. Jessica followed and slipped into the closet after me.

"Got you," she said.

"You're not It," I replied.

"Really?"

I pushed my shirts back against the wall, giving us more room to stand. Still, it was impossible to keep from touching. "You aren't avoiding me, are you?" she asked. A sliver of light streamed through the crack between the doors, illuminating one side of her face.

"No," I said. "Why would I avoid you?"

"Fee . . . fi . . . fo . . . fum," called Dickie from somewhere out in the room.

We tried to be quiet, but he must have known where we were. Instead of opening the closet and tagging us, Dickie jammed the door shut and fiddled with the latch.

"Shit!" I said, shoving the door.

A moment later, I heard the padlock click shut. Dickie drummed on the closet. "You two behave," he said.

"Hey, wait!" I called, but it was too late. He'd already run off to find someone else. I glanced at Jessica. "Sorry. He's kind of . . ."

Jessica put her finger to my mouth. Then she kissed me, biting my lip in a way that stung and made me shiver all at once. "There," she said. "Your move."

My arms trembled. I tried to remember how to kiss from that truth-or-dare game I'd played in middle school, but this was completely different. Jessica kissed like she wanted to devour me. I leaned toward her, not sure if I should open or close my eyes or how to turn my head.

"Like this," she said, pulling me against her. She kissed

me so gently I could barely feel her lips brushing mine. Her mouth slid from my mouth to my neck, and down to the muscle that sloped to my shoulder. Then she bit me, making me all shivery again.

I got the hang of it after a few more tries, letting my lips move playfully over hers.

Jessica took my hand and squeezed it. "You're the one," she whispered.

"The one what?"

"The one who's going to sink me."

I wanted to ask what that meant, but I was afraid of seeming dumb. "Okay," I said, and kissed her again, inhaling the bubble-gum scent of her hair.

After a little while, Mike's calls of "No babies!" trickled in from the hall.

"Crap," I whispered. My elbow thumped the back of the closet. Dickie returned just in time, fumbled with the lock, and let us out.

Jessica straightened her shirt and gave me a wink. "See you, J.T."

I stood, wide-eyed and smiling, as she left. No one from my old school would ever believe I'd kissed a girl like Jessica Keen.

Dickie shook his head and chuckled. "See? Told you she was into you."

"You're such a jerk," I said, unable to keep a ridiculous grin off my face.

He slapped my back. "You're welcome."

Tools of the Trade

THAT NIGHT I FOUGHT *my first demon.*

Kiana showed me how to strap the sword to my back and wrap a scarf around my head to hide my face. "There's a war going on," she said, pulling her own scarf over her mouth and nose. "If you want to live, you have to stay hidden. Not everyone here's your friend."

I followed them through the maze of streets. We passed other figures wearing scarfs, but none spoke or gave me a second look. Nick stopped at a narrow alley. He cocked his head, as if listening for something. "It's down there," he whispered.

Kiana handed me a coil of silver cable. "Tools of the trade," she said.

"What am I supposed to do?"

"Simple. Hunt the demons before they hunt you."

I peered into the alley. It went on for fifty feet or so before it got too dark to see farther. A low slurping, like the sound of a dog drinking, reverberated off the walls.

Kiana fixed the cable to a strap on my hip. "The sword will work, but demons can't be killed," she explained. "You have to use the cable to bind them. Understand?"

"Sure."

"We'll see about that," Nick muttered.

"I got it," I said, eager to prove myself.

I held the sword before me and entered the alley. Puddles of oily liquid dappled the ground, and the brick walls shimmered with moisture. The buildings seemed to lean closer, surrounding me as I walked toward the slurping sound.

My eyes still hadn't adjusted to the dark when I heard the thudding steps of something approaching. A demon burst out of the shadows, resembling a sumo wrestler crawling on all fours. Instinctively, I swung my sword at its reaching arm.

Hot blood splattered my cheeks. The demon reared and bellowed, its arm completely severed. For a moment I felt triumphant, then two more arms—thinner, wormier ones—writhed out of the bleeding stump.

It came at me again. I slashed its arms and legs, but the more I injured it, the more limbs it grew. My confidence vanished. All I could think about was fighting harder, hurting it more. I stabbed the demon's eye, and tentacles wormed out of the wound, entangling my hand. My sword clattered to the ground as more tentacles grabbed my legs and chest.

The creature lifted me toward its slobbering mouth. I reached for my sword, only it was too far away. Something I'd heard once floated through my head—that if you died in a dream, you'd die in real life. Panic surged through me, filling me with desperate strength, but still I couldn't free myself from the tentacles.

My hand brushed the cable at my waist. I grabbed a length and looped it around the demon's head, trying to strangle him with it. The metal tightened like a thin silver snake. Instantly, the demon dropped me, clawing at the cable.

I hurried to bind the demon's limbs. Everywhere the cable touched, it seemed to stick to the creature's skin. Pulling back, I pinned its arms to its sides, then I looped more cable around its legs and tentacles until at last the demon fell.

With a snap, the end of the cable broke free, leaving the demon cocooned in a tangle of silver braid. I glanced at the creature's chubby bulldog face. It whimpered, looking more pitiful now than terrifying. I almost wanted to release it, but I knew it would come at me again.

The sound of clapping startled me from my thoughts.

"Took you long enough," Nick said. "I thought you were dinner."

I wiped the creature's blood off my brow.

Kiana smiled. "Don't listen to him, J.T. That was good for your first time." She slung her arm around my waist and steered me away from the body.

We'd almost reached the street when a dull chittering filled the alley, making my skin prickle. A tall, insectlike figure with a long mosquito mouth stepped out of the shadows behind us. The demon's struggles grew more frantic as the figure approached it.

"What's that?" I asked.

"Just a Nomanchulator," Kiana said.

"Nothing to worry about," Nick added. "It'll take care of the body."

The Nomanchulator squatted on too-thin legs. Its mouth hovered over the demon's chest.

Kiana tugged my shirt. "We should get going."

I couldn't move. The Nomanchulator's dead black eyes glanced at me and a wide, clownish leer warped its face. Then it plunged its mouth into the demon, like a spider eating a caught fly.

I turned, wishing I hadn't looked.

ghosT PacT

ghost44: Hey, sex god.

johnnyrotten: You're a girl, right?

ghost44: Last time I checked.

johnnyrotten: You don't write like a girl.

ghost44: I don't throw like a girl either.

johnnyrotten: I mean, you use caps and complete sentences and all that.

ghost44: would u prefer i write 2u like this? ;)

johnnyrotten: I'll pass.

ghost44: I should have been born into a different time. I'm not much for abbreviation and emoticons and all that fluff. I miss letters—long, old-fashioned, beautifully written letters where people poured their hearts out and used words like "beholden" and "protean."

johnnyrotten: Protean?

ghost44: Constantly changing. Taking on different shapes, forms, meanings, etc. As in, "I am beholden to your protean heart."

johnnyrotten: So why don't you write me a letter?

ghost44: No attention span for it. Besides, it's lonely writing letters. You spend all your time trying to capture some fleeting, gut-wrenching feeling in words, and then you never even know if the person you send it to reads it. Or what they're doing when they read it. Or if they understand. There's no feedback. Rather narcissistic when you think about it. I mean, who's the letter for—yourself or the person you're writing to? At least this way, I know you're there.

johnnyrotten: Yeah, but I could be picking my nose right now or sitting buck naked while feral wombats lick pudding off my chest.

ghost44: That's how I prefer to see you—except with chocolate syrup instead of pudding.

johnnyrotten: Great. Wish I knew how to see you. Why are you afraid to tell me who you are?

ghost44: That again? If you keep asking who I am, you're missing the point.

johnnyrotten: Hold up. I'm not asking *who* anymore.

ghost44: You're not?

johnnyrotten: Nope. I'm asking *why.* As in, Why bother with this secrecy? Why not tell me your name?

ghost44: That's easy. You ever curse at a dog in a sweet voice?

johnnyrotten: WTF???

ghost44: Most of the time, that's all people do when they talk to each other. Take the phrase: "Your hair looks nice." Or

"Pretty dress." Or "You want to work on chemistry homework together?" Translation: "That style is lame." "You're such a slut." "What will it take to get in your pants?"

johnnyrotten: Are you saying that when I do homework with my lab partners, I really want to sleep with them?

ghost44: No. But when you *ask* to do homework with someone, is it because you really want to solve equations with them?

johnnyrotten: I see your point.

ghost44: Communication is deception. What I'm offering is a far better thing.

johnnyrotten: So what are you offering?

ghost44: Something honest. Conversation without all the lies.

johnnyrotten: People don't always lie. Sometimes they say what they mean.

ghost44: Oh please. You, of all people, know better.

johnnyrotten: What's that supposed to mean?

ghost44: Just that everyone's concerned about their image. Everyone wants to seem a certain way. Act a certain way. Fit in. Be popular.

johnnyrotten: I don't care about my image.

ghost44: Yes, you do. It's just part of your image to seem like you don't care.

johnnyrotten: And you're so much better?

ghost44: No. I'm worse. I'm consumed by image—that's why I'm a ghost. It's only when I have no image at all that I can be honest.

johnnyrotten: Hold up. How is talking online any more honest than talking to someone in person? I mean, for all I know, you could be a forty-year-old trucker who hacked into our server and is pretending to be a seventeen-year-old girl.

ghost44: You think I'm forty? How mature of me! Actually, I'm a six-year-old whiz kid in India and I'm writing you during recess to improve my English.

johnnyrotten: Now I'm disturbed.

ghost44: The point is, it doesn't matter what my name is. Image, popularity, dress size—all of that is completely irrelevant, because here we're just words. Sure I could lie to you and pretend to be someone else, but why bother? If I'm free to be anyone, then I'm free to be myself. My true self. That's what I mean by honest.

johnnyrotten: So what do you mean by "true self"?

ghost44: Mmmm . . . don't know yet, but I'd like to find out. I'll make you a deal. A ghost pact.

johnnyrotten: Go on.

ghost44: I'll promise to be as soul-strippingly, mind-shatteringly honest as I can be, if you'll do the same.

johnnyrotten: Deal. Just one more *why* question.

ghost44: Shoot.

johnnyrotten: Why me?

ghost44: Because, dear James, you need to be honest with someone.

Danger Golf

"I HEARD YOU AND JESSICA KEEN hooked up," Frank Wood announced in his typical booming voice. It was a few minutes before physics class started, and Dr. Choi hadn't arrived yet. "Concerned citizens want to know: what happened in the closet?"

"Dude, what do you think?" I replied, glancing at Ellie. She pulled a notebook out of her backpack and slapped it onto her desk.

"Oh, man," Frank said, his eyes widening. "So are you two going out?"

"I don't know."

Frank nodded. "Right. I get it." Then he gave me a sly, guy-to-guy look. "That's cool."

Dr. Choi walked in and Frank hurried back to his desk, but his question kept nagging me. I really didn't know what to make of Jess and me. We hadn't talked since

Friday. When I saw her at lunch, sitting at her usual table, she didn't wave me over or leave her group to sit with me, and I didn't cross the cafeteria to join her.

It wasn't until a few nights later, while I was out chipping golf balls with a five iron during social hour, that Jess came up to me. Dickie was off with Sunny somewhere, and Heinous was playing video games. I wasn't a big fan of golf, but chipping balls gave me an excuse to walk around alone outside without looking like a loser.

"I always thought golf was something bald guys with beer bellies did," Jess said as she approached.

"Not danger golf," I replied. "Danger golf's different." I explained how the object of danger golf was to hit the ball in a random direction without breaking anything. It was the sort of game I figured I'd play, even though I never had.

Jessica pointed me toward the tennis courts. "Okay, hotshot. Go for it."

I lined up and took a full swing. The ball landed smack in the middle of the far court and bounced over the fence.

"Want to give it a try?"

"Sure," she said. "But I don't know how to swing."

I tossed out a ball and passed her the club. "It's easy." With my hands on hers, I guided her through a swing. "See?"

We swung together, my arms wrapped around her body and my cheek brushing hers. After a few swings, she took her hand off the club and touched the inside of my forearm. The cuts I'd given myself had healed, leaving raised, pink scars. "How'd you get these?" she asked.

I pulled my arm back. "Fighting," I said. "I used to fight a lot."

"Really?" She sounded skeptical.

"Really."

"Who'd you fight?"

"Other kids. Jerks mostly."

"Did they carry knives or something?"

"Not exactly."

"What does that mean?"

I hesitated, hoping she'd drop it and let the scars be a mystery.

"Come on. You can tell me," she pressed.

"Swear you'll never tell anyone?"

"Yeah."

I pointed to a few scars and described the street fights that had caused them. Some details I invented, and some I pulled from the fights in my dreams. Jess seemed to buy it.

"Sounds like fun," she said.

"Not really," I replied. "But it was exciting."

"My man." She brushed her fingers along my arm.

My cheeks burned. I felt a little funny that she believed me. Then again, it wasn't that far from the truth. What difference did it make if I cut myself or if someone else cut me?

I pointed to the ball. "You have to hit it as hard as you can. Them's the rules, missy."

"No problem." Jess lined up and swung. She lifted her head, so the ball didn't go far. I gave her a few pointers and her second shot was a beauty. The ball landed in the bleachers, hitting the metal with a loud *thunk!*

"Pretty good," I said.

"I'm a fast learner."

We went back and forth, daring each other to hit balls toward riskier targets. At one point, Jess pointed me directly at the faculty parking lot. I got under the ball, so it went high and came down next to Hassert's van. Luckily, it took an odd bounce and rolled away.

Jess told me all about how she'd grown up in the city sneaking into clubs and watching shows. When she was fourteen, she could pass for twenty-one. She talked about bands that I'd never heard of, and how she wanted to be a DJ. In addition to knowing a lot about music, she'd played a few concerts herself. Not rock concerts, though. Jess played classical piano. "Mozart's pretty hard-core," she said. "Seriously. Put in the third movement of Mozart's Requiem Mass, crank it up, and tell me you don't want to thrash your head and slam someone. Chopin is good, too."

I pictured her onstage in her black combat boots and fishnet stockings, blowing the stodgy audience away. "Maybe sometime I can hear you play," I said.

"Sure. You'd be amazed by what I can do with my hands."

I duffed the ball I was supposed to hit toward the school. Then Jess took the same shot and chipped it onto the roof. After that, we had to look for some of the balls we'd already hit.

"So besides fighting, what do you do?" she asked.

"I write letters," I said. "Long, gut-wrenching, protean letters."

"Protean letters? What's that mean?" She gave me a coy smile. I wondered if she really didn't know what I was talking about, or if this was part of her game. "Are you one of those geeks who spends all his time in chat rooms?" she asked.

"Could be."

"That doesn't sound very exciting."

"Depends who you're writing to."

"I guess." Jess glanced away, as if avoiding something.

The silence became awkward. I thought of what ghost44 had said, about how she could only be herself in secret. I didn't want to risk losing her by asking too much, so instead I changed the subject. "I've also been in thirteen car accidents," I lied.

She laughed. "Thirteen?"

"Well, they weren't exactly accidents."

"You mean they were intentional?"

"Call it purposefully accidental. My friends and I would borrow cars and drive them to the country to do

Dukes of Hazzard moves. On dirt roads, I could usually pull a few 360s."

"Remind me to never let you drive."

"I'm a good driver. Most people don't know how to crash. But I like crashing."

"Me, too." Jess smiled mischievously. "I'm all about crashing." She tossed me a ball and pointed to her dorm. "Your turn."

I hit a beautiful shot. The ball arced, becoming a tiny white speck as it floated toward a second-floor window.

"Uh-oh . . ." I muttered.

The sound of breaking glass echoed across campus like a starter's pistol. We sprinted to the pond, and I tossed the club into the water. Then we ducked behind some bushes near the cleavage. Lights flicked on as security guards and RCs streamed out of the dorms like angry ants.

"Crap! Crap! Crap!" I said.

Jess giggled and kissed me. "So we blend in," she whispered, glancing at another couple that was walking the pond.

We kept kissing. My heart beat so crazily I could feel the blood thumping through my veins.

"I like this game," she said.

Donuts

ghost44: Knock knock.

johnnyrotten: Nice try, but I'm not going to ask you who you are anymore.

ghost44: Really? Have you finally moved beyond such superficial things?

johnnyrotten: Nope. I figured it out.

ghost44: You did?

johnnyrotten: Yup. I know who you are. Only I've decided to keep it a secret.

ghost44: If you wanted to keep it a secret, then why tell me that you know?

johnnyrotten: Because—I like this game.

ghost44: All right, Mr. Know-It-All, let's play another game. Questions. I'll answer one of your questions if you'll answer one of mine. But no *who* questions.

johnnyrotten: Do I go first?

ghost44: Yes. My turn.

johnnyrotten: Hold up. That doesn't count.

ghost44: It was a question. Rules are rules.

johnnyrotten: Bring it on.

ghost44: Do you like Jessica Keen?

johnnyrotten: I can't imagine why you'd ask that.

ghost44: So what's your answer?

johnnyrotten: Depends what you mean by "like."

ghost44: Put it this way. Do you (a) lust after her hot body, (b) enjoy messing around with her, (c) like the idea of being with her, or (d) love her?

johnnyrotten: That's totally unfair.

ghost44: Quit stalling.

johnnyrotten: OK. I think she's cool.

ghost44: That wasn't one of the choices.

johnnyrotten: I'm rebellious like that. My turn. Tell me something about you that no one else knows.

ghost44: Nice question.

johnnyrotten: So?

ghost44: How about this—My mom hates me.

johnnyrotten: For real?

ghost44: Yup. She won't say it directly, and no one ever talks about it, but she does.

johnnyrotten: Why?

ghost44: You'd have to meet my mom to get that.

johnnyrotten: Describe her.

ghost44: Hmmm . . . Basically, she's wealthy, successful, and perfect in every way. She even had the perfect divorce. In fact,

the only thing that's not perfect in her life is me. I'm the one
piece that won't fit her puzzle, so I ruin the whole thing.

johnnyrotten: Sounds familiar.

ghost44: Are your parents divorced?

johnnyrotten: No. But I used to wish they were.

ghost44: Why?

johnnyrotten: Is that your question?

ghost44: Yes.

johnnyrotten: I guess I thought that if one of them moved
away, my life would be more interesting.

ghost44: Trust me: having two toothbrushes isn't all it's
cracked up to be.

johnnyrotten: That's not what I mean.

ghost44: Then what do you mean?

johnnyrotten: It's hard to explain. Do you ever wish you could
be someone else?

ghost44: Sometimes. Mostly, though, I wish I could be myself.

johnnyrotten: Why can't you?

ghost44: Because I'm not good enough.

johnnyrotten: Why not?

ghost44: I'm just not. Anyhow, it's my turn.

ghost44: What's your favorite childhood memory?

johnnyrotten: Running away. Yours?

ghost44: Sunday mornings eating donuts with my dad.

johnnyrotten: Mmm . . . donuts.

ghost44: He'd let me order anything I wanted. Cinnamon
twists. Chocolate éclairs. The ones with the colored sprinkles
on top. Sometimes I'd take a bite of each and leave the rest,

and he didn't care if I made a mess. It was the only day of the week that he didn't work.

johnnyrotten: I like that.

ghost44: So tell me about running away.

johnnyrotten: Hold on.

johnnyrotten: I need to go. My RC is calling me over for a wing meeting.

ghost44: Wait!

johnnyrotten: ?

ghost44: Be careful, okay?

johnnyrotten: Be careful of what?

ghost44: Stay a ghost for too long and you might disappear.

WINning

I FOUGHT MORE DEMONS in my dreams. It wasn't every night—maybe once or twice a week. Some had claws, hair, and jagged teeth like animals, and some were almost human yet wrong. There were clowns with shark teeth. Hyena men. Fire-haired witches with snakeskin arms. A cat that changed into a corpse-pale girl whose eyes were bloodred pits. They terrified me, but I learned to control my fear and shape my dreams.

The only thing I couldn't face were the Nomanchulators. Every time I bound a demon, Nomanchulators scuttled out of the cracks and shadows to feed off the body. I tried not to look at them, but the sound of their chittering as they dragged the demons away made my spine numb.

It seemed like the more I fought, the more numerous the Nomanchulators became.

"You're doing good," Kiana said one night after I'd bound a particularly nasty alligator demon. She must have sensed my disgust over the Nomanchulators. "Keep this up, and it won't be long until you win this war."

"And then what?" I asked.

"Then you can do whatever you like." She grinned. "You'll have total control, and you won't need to struggle anymore."

"So who's left to fight?" I asked.

"Don't get ahead of yourself, hotshot," Nick interrupted. "These are the easy ones." He sniffed the air, as if he could smell the demons out there waiting to attack. "The hardest part is yet to come."

Black Ops

DICKIE WANTED ME TO SLIP OUT after curfew with him and spend the night in the girls' dorm. He talked about the mission for almost a week, trying to get me on board. Every time he brought it up, I'd nod and say something like "I wish," but sneaking over to the girls' dorm after curfew was no easy feat. For starters, all the doors in the dorms had security cards that recorded whenever anyone went in or out. Leaving your dorm after curfew earned you an automatic suspension. On top of that, every dorm had an RC on duty throughout the night and there were security guards who patrolled the campus, so even if we made it out, we'd still have to cross the open, well-lit space between dorms without being seen. Every year, some desperate guy got busted trying to sneak into his girlfriend's room.

The way Dickie pitched it, the risk only made things better, as if running across a strip of minimally landscaped ground in the middle of the night would make us heroes. "Trust me," he said. "If we go, it'll be well worth it."

It wasn't only the chance of getting suspended that bothered me. The prospect of spending the night in Jess's room made me anxious for reasons I couldn't name. Granted, she was completely hot and I wanted to be with her. Yet part of me felt a little weird about it, too, like maybe I was doing it for the wrong reasons—which is totally not the way guys are supposed to think. At any rate, I couldn't let Dickie see my apprehensions. Rebels have to be raring to go, regardless of the consequences.

"I talked with Sunny and she's game," Dickie said during lunch one day. "So what do you say, amigo? You up for some black ops this Friday?"

"Hell, yeah," I said, struggling to swallow my Tater Tots. "Except, I'm not sure if Jess is. We've only been together a few weeks and I don't want to seem too eager, you know?"

Dickie nodded. "Give her time. Pretend that sex is the last thing on your mind and she'll beg you to come over."

"Right-o. Like maybe I'm questioning my sexuality and she needs to convert me."

"Don't laugh," he replied. "It works."

We kept joking about new ways to get girls to proposition us, like pretending to be ultrareligious and beyond temptation, or brokenhearted poets, or sheltered virgins who needed to be taught the ways of love. I'd never told Dickie that I actually was a virgin. He seemed to assume that I'd done it before, so I bluffed my way through most conversations. It was like we shared this secret understanding of girls that Heinous and the other sophs in our wing weren't privy to. When social hour rolled around, we headed out together—the studs of Dingo wing, off to meet Jess and Sunny and mess around by the pond while Heinous stayed inside with Cheese and played video games.

Dickie mentioned sneaking out again the next day, but I distracted him by bringing up the Steves and how they kept gloating over slaughtering us with water balloons. I convinced him that our honor needed to be avenged, so we set to work on a plan to get the Steves back. We didn't deliberately exclude Heinous, but since the Steves were roommates, it seemed fitting to keep participation limited to just us—that way it could be roommates versus roommates.

When the Steves were out playing basketball that evening, we broke into their room with a coat hanger. Dickie set up a few standard pranks—plastic wrap on the toilet, baby powder on their pillows—but these were merely diversionary tactics. The real prank was what we did to their shower. Inspired by *Psycho*, I unscrewed the shower nozzle and stuffed it full of cotton soaked in red food coloring, then screwed it back on. Meanwhile, Dickie stole their soap so they wouldn't be able to wash away the food coloring. To top things off, he emptied the only bottle of shampoo (the Steves shared shampoo!) and refilled it with vegetable oil.

It worked brilliantly. In chemistry class the following day, Steve Dennon's normally pale face glowed red and his hair dripped oil onto his shirt. Steve Lacone, on the other hand, obviously hadn't dared to shower at all. Baby powder still dusted his wavy black hair. I had to hold my breath to keep from laughing.

After the prank succeeded, Dickie pushed the idea of sneaking into the girls' dorm more. He let the plan drop around Jess in the hall between classes. "Hell, yeah!" she said. "You boys better come over."

"You're in, superstud," Dickie told me afterward. "The ladies await."

I slapped his hand and faked excitement. There was no way to back out now.

Friday night, we stayed in our dorm room until after Mike went around for eleven PM check-in. As soon as he was gone, we stuffed our beds with pillows and dressed like ninjas—black pants, black hoodies, black socks, and shoes. Dickie grabbed some condoms in foil packets from the teapot he kept near his bed. "Need some?" he asked. "Boy Scouts are always prepared, right?"

I slipped a couple foil packets into my back pocket without looking at them.

Dickie checked his watch and called Sunny. "Five minutes till launch, Sunshine," he told her. "Keep a lookout. Flick the lights if you see trouble."

We opened our door, careful to stop the latch from clicking. Hassert had night duty. Normally, he stayed in the office watching TV, but sometimes he wandered the halls, pounding on doors if he heard anyone talking. "Shut your yap traps," he'd say, like he was some badass drill sergeant.

We had to sneak down to Heinous and Cheese's room, since they lived on the first floor and there was no way to dangle out our second-story window without being spotted by a security guard. Dickie tapped a code on the door, and Heinous let us in.

Their room smelled funky, like athlete's foot spray and soggy Cheetos. That's how Cheese got his nickname. His fingers and clothes were permanently stained orange from constantly eating bags of puffed cheese. Even though Cheese acted like a perverted koala—sleepy, sex-crazed, and harmless—he was wicked smart. He'd scored a perfect 240 on his PSATs. Then, on a dare, he'd taken the real SATs while completely drunk and missed only one question. The weird thing was, he almost never did homework, so his grades sucked. He mostly slept—twelve hours a day.

Cheese rubbed his eyes and groaned when we came in. "All my money's in my underwear," he said.

"Nothing's happening," Dickie said. "Go back to sleep."

"Oh, yeah," Cheese muttered. "I'll show you sleep."

We kept the lights off and looked out the window. "Well, boys," Heinous said, like a general addressing his troops, "tonight you go where few have gone before. If you survive, you'll be men. But it could get rough out there, so if you need me to take your place . . ."

"Dream on," Dickie said.

I peered out the window for security guards. At least one usually patrolled campus, and part of me clung to the hope that he might be camped between our dorm and the girls', forcing us to call things off. No such luck, though. Dickie spotted the security guard on his normal rounds, walking between two dorms at the far end of the quad. "Here comes our opening," he said.

We waited for the guard to disappear behind a wall before climbing out. Heinous slid the window shut after us.

On three, Dickie and I bolted across the expanse of grass between dorms. I never ran so fast in my life, practically diving to the ground once I reached the girls' dorm. Dickie crawled to the base of what he thought was Sunny's window and tapped the glass while I struggled to catch my breath. If an RC looked out, we were screwed beyond belief.

After a long, freaky silence, the window slid open. "You there?" Sunny whispered.

"Right-o," Dickie said, popping up.

I gave him a boost. Once he crawled in, he leaned out

and gave me a hand. Sunny closed the blinds after us like a pro.

"Hey," she said to me.

"Hey," I replied, my voice tight.

"You made it," Jess crooned. She wrapped her arms around my neck and kissed me. "You kids have fun," she said to Dickie and Sunny, then she led me to her room on the second floor. She didn't bother checking for RCs or stopping the doors from clicking, as if being bold was enough to keep us from getting busted.

"Where's Rachel?" I asked once we were safe in her room.

"I kicked her out for the night. She understands."

Jess lit a few candles and dimmed the lights. I sat on her bed, careful not to hit my head on the top bunk.

"I wondered if you'd come," she said.

"I told you I would."

"There's a difference between what people say and what they do." She slid off her shoes and sat beside me. "I'm impressed—that's all."

"It's nothing. I've done far more dangerous things than this."

"I bet." She stared at me, but didn't say anything else.

"So, are you tired?" I asked.

"A little."

"Do you want to go to sleep?"

"What do you think?"

I glanced at her walls, feigning interest in her music posters. "I like your room. Are all these posters yours?"

"You are such a dork."

I opened my mouth to explain why I thought her posters were cool, but before I could, Jess pushed me back and straddled my waist. The plastic condom wrappers in my pocket crinkled. "What's that?"

"Nothing," I said.

She narrowed her eyes and slid her hand into my pocket, fishing out the condoms. "Expecting something, mister?"

"No." My face flushed. "I, uh . . . They're not really mine."

She tossed the condoms onto her desk. "That's the worst excuse I've ever heard."

"It's true."

She laughed and kissed me. "I've got better ones," she whispered, pulling off my shirt.

I started to pull off hers, but I forgot to unbutton the top. "Very slick," she said. "How about I take off the bra?"

"I've got it." I fiddled with the back clasp with one hand, only it wouldn't come undone.

Jess smirked. "Try two hands, hotshot."

I did, but those little hooks were impossible. She finally reached around and undid her bra with a smooth, easy flick.

"How'd you do that?"

"One of the mysteries of being a girl." She leaned over me, her skin warm against mine.

My gaze kept drifting to her chest. I acted like I was only interested in her tattoo, brushing my fingers down her cleavage, over the black lines in her smooth skin. There were five Japanese characters, each slightly larger than a quarter. Before, I'd only seen the first two characters and the top half of the third, but now I could see all five, nestled between the slopes of her bare breasts.

"Is this your first time?" she asked.

"No." My voice cracked. "How about you?"

Jess chuckled. "Very funny."

She kissed my neck and unsnapped my jeans, so I unsnapped hers. Then she slid her pants over the curve of her hips, pulling her legs free one at a time. It was a lot like danger golf—like we were daring each other to go further. I struggled out of my jeans, bumping the wall with my elbow.

Jess paused, wearing only her black underwear. Images from movies shuffled through my head. What came next? Kiss her? Slide my hand up her leg? Say something manly?

Luckily, Jess took over, placing my hands on her hips and moving against me.

Even though I'd fantasized about sex for years, now that it was actually happening, it was different from what I'd expected. I mean, it felt intense, yet part of me kept getting distracted, so I couldn't fully experience the intensity. *This is it,* I told myself, *I'm in bed with Jessica Keen,* but telling myself that only took me one step further from feeling it.

I closed my eyes and tried to imagine being with Jess, which was weird, since I actually was with her. Then I opened my eyes, but I didn't know where to look. My gaze finally settled on her chest, tracing the lines of her tattoo. I pictured her lying on a padded table while some guy carved those symbols into her bare skin with needle and ink. She'd probably used a fake ID, because she wasn't yet eighteen. I wondered what the Japanese characters meant and why they were so important to her that she'd want them etched between her breasts, near her heart. Together, the five characters resembled a ladder. It reminded me of a passage from *The Great Gatsby* that I'd read recently—the one where Gatsby is walking with Daisy and he looks at the lines on the sidewalk and thinks of them as a ladder that he could climb to a place where everything would be exactly the way he'd always imagined it. Except a few of the black lines tattooed on Jess's chest were diagonal, so if it was a ladder, some of the rungs must have been broken.

Jess bit me, bringing me out of my thoughts. Why the hell was I thinking about *The Great Gatsby* when she was right there? Naked. I tried again to focus on her. Things got more intense, but only distantly, like my body was having sex in a different room from my mind. Our breathing picked up until at last we collapsed against each other.

Her hair, damp with sweat, stuck to my cheek. I wasn't certain if that was it, only there was no way to ask without sounding stupid.

"Was that okay?" I whispered.

She drew back to look at me, and I liked her then. I really did. Because I could tell she was just as lost as me, even though she hid it well.

I wanted to laugh and say something about how that wasn't what I'd expected. Something about how I could never get the world inside my head to fit with the world outside. But I couldn't think of a way to say it without offending her. "It's like *The Great Gatsby*," I whispered.

"You're a strange egg," she said.

Jess pulled on her shirt and curled with her back to me.

After a while, I fell asleep.

aNimaL LonELiness

ghost44: You there?

johnnyrotten: I think so.

ghost44: The strangest thing happened today. I was walking to class when I saw a squirrel touching a crow.

johnnyrotten: Like, eating it? Killer squirrel on the loose?

ghost44: No, sicko. The two of them were huddled near those bushes by the gym, calm as could be. The squirrel stroked the crow's feathers, and the crow rubbed its beak against the squirrel's shoulder. I'm not kidding. When they saw me, they broke apart like lovers caught kissing.

johnnyrotten: Weird.

ghost44: Do you think animals get lonely?

johnnyrotten: Sure.

ghost44: No one ever talks about it.

johnnyrotten: About what? Animal loneliness? If that's what you're into, there're probably some websites you could visit.

ghost44: No, pervy. No one ever talks about IT.

johnnyrotten: What's "IT"?

ghost44: The things that matter. What's at the center. People talk and talk, but they never say much. Sometimes we get close, but we rarely mention the truth.

johnnyrotten: What truth?

ghost44: That no one ever really knows anyone else.

johnnyrotten: That's depressing.

ghost44: That's the way it is.

johnnyrotten: So why bother talking? Why bother messaging me?

ghost44: Because I saw a squirrel touching a crow today.

ghost44: You still there?

johnnyrotten: Yeah. I was just thinking about that.

ghost44: I heard you spent the night at Jess's place.

johnnyrotten: How do you know these things?

ghost44: I have my supernatural sources. I didn't think you'd do that.

johnnyrotten: Are you pissed at me?

ghost44: A little. Do you like her?

johnnyrotten: If I tell you, will you promise not to tell anyone?

ghost44: Who could I tell? No one can see me.

johnnyrotten: She's cool. She's like my dream girl.

ghost44: Lucky you.

johnnyrotten: I know. I should be happy.

ghost44: But?

johnnyrotten: But . . . it's like this cheap plastic magic trick I had as a kid—the one where you put a quarter in the slot and slide it shut. Then you turn it around and open it and presto! The quarter's gone.

ghost44: I had one of those. It was purple.

johnnyrotten: Mine was green, only something broke in it so I could never get the quarter to come back.

ghost44: What does a broken magic trick have to do with Jess the wonder girl?

johnnyrotten: That's how I feel when I'm with her. Everything should be right. I put the quarter in the slot and the audience is waiting expectantly, but I keep coming up empty.

ghost44: Guess you don't think I'm Jessica Keen anymore.

johnnyrotten: No. Definitely not.

ghost44: What makes you so sure?

johnnyrotten: Because the only time I don't get that empty feeling is when I'm messaging you.

ghost44: Thanks.

johnnyrotten: For what?

ghost44: For finally talking about *IT*.

The Burrows

"TIME TO COMPLETE YOUR TRAINING," *Nick said, opening the door to a small, dingy room. "Think you've beaten most of the demons out there?"*

"I have."

He shook his head. "The hard ones have all gone underground. To kill a weed, you've got to pull up its roots."

"How?"

Nick nodded to a bed in the corner. "Go to sleep."

"I am asleep."

"Then go to sleep again," Kiana said, patting the mattress. "Go deeper."

I sat on the bed. When I lay back, the room changed, morphing into my dorm room with a bunk bed above me and my closet behind me. Posters covered the walls, and papers cluttered my desk.

"What you see is largely a matter of expectation," Kiana explained. "It's easiest to think of an elevator, though. That way, you can keep track of how far down you go."

I nodded and closed my eyes.

After a while, I dreamed I was in an elevator. The old-fashioned arrow above the doors rotated down a notch. With a ding, the doors slid open, revealing a nightclub pulsing with music and movement.

"Welcome to the burrows," Nick said, stepping out of the elevator. "Now things get interesting."

Kiana took my hand and led me across the dance floor. Compared to the quiet emptiness of the surface level, the burrows were mesmerizing. A woman with horns writhed against a blue-masked angel while white-faced mimes blew fire and a jester juggled rats. There were people with wings, monkeys, minotaurs, and knights in armor. A tall, chubby rabbit stood behind the bar, performing magic tricks.

The guides surveyed the room, looking for someone. Nick finally pointed to a figure by the far wall. A pale scarf covered his face, and an elegant white-handled sword hung off his side.

"That's White Blade," he said. "If you want to win, he's the one you have to beat."

The white-cloaked figure must have noticed us staring, because he turned suddenly and headed for the door. I started after him, pushing through the crowd.

"Let him go," said a woman blocking the doorway.

She seemed familiar, although I couldn't figure out why. "Who are you?"

"I'm the Thief."

I frowned, confused. Before I could ask anything else, Nick was telling her to get out of our way. The Thief reached for my shoulder, but Nick knocked her arm aside. Quick as a blink, she spun, catching his jaw with the back of her hand.

The two of them traded blows and blocks like fighters in a kung-fu movie. Whoever the Thief was, she clearly had power. Nick was no small entity, but he could barely hold her off.

"Go!" he grunted, glancing at me. "Don't lose him!"

I stood, not sure who to trust.

"Hunt the demons before they hunt you," Kiana urged.

It made sense. If I didn't go after White Blade, he'd come after me. I had to protect myself.

I slipped out of the nightclub and into the alley

where White Blade had gone. As I turned a corner, a silver blur sliced toward my face. I ducked, and the sword whooshed past, lodging into the bricks behind me.

White Blade kicked my chest, and my breath huffed out. Then his fist struck my jaw. I crumpled to the ground, losing control. Blood tickled my cheek. The more he hit me, the less it hurt.

Kiana must have seen that I'd lost my grip. "Wake up!" she shouted from farther back in the alley.

A foot smashed my face, and my mouth filled with blood. I ran my tongue over the jagged end of a chipped tooth. Great, I thought. That'll look nice.

Another blow made my senses scatter. Everything was falling apart. First thing in the morning I'll have to call a dentist.

My mind seized on that thought. Morning. In the morning. *White Blade pulled his sword free and raised it over my head.*

I woke.

My head lay on a pillow. I kicked off the hot, sticky sheets. Just a dream, *I told myself, relieved that I'd made it out. My tongue flicked over the edge of my teeth, finding the front one chipped. Pain surged through my jaw from the exposed nerve. I touched my face, and my fingers came away wet with blood.*

A sword slid between the elevator doors, prying them apart.

Panic gripped me. Then I remembered that I'd fallen asleep twice—it was still a dream. Wake up, damn it! *I hissed, slapping my cheeks. The pain from my tooth became excruciating.*

My chest seized, and my eyes flicked open. The room appeared gray. I stared at the pattern of springs on the mattress above me. Touching my face felt no more real than it had in the dream, except there was no blood. Still, my jaw ached.

The clock on my desk said it was 5:47 AM, but I didn't want to risk going back to sleep. I staggered to the bathroom. My breath caught when I looked in the mirror.

Black lines stained my face. Written in large block letters across my forehead were the words BEAT ME.

ELfed

THE MARKER MUST HAVE BEEN permanent, because no matter how much I scrubbed, it didn't come off. Dickie had lines on his face, too, but not nearly as bad as mine. I guess that was the advantage of sleeping on the top bunk.

I tried wearing a bandanna low across my forehead, except it made me look like a demented hippie. Dickie decided to pretend everything was normal and let other people freak about it. Easy for him to do—he didn't have any words on his forehead (although they had colored the tip of his nose red, and I noticed that he tried very hard to get *that* off).

The best I could do was to scribble over the "B" with another magic marker so instead of BEAT ME it said EAT ME. It wasn't much, but I thought it made a better statement.

By the end of first period, at least a hundred students had asked about my forehead. I started making up ridiculous stories to explain it. I said it was a political statement, and I said it wasn't marker, but a tattoo. Then I told Beth Lindbergh, who was incredibly gullible, that it was how they marked admission at this nightclub in Chicago, and I made her swear not to tell anyone I'd snuck off campus to go there. She nodded, taking it very seriously.

In a way, the nightclub story felt the most true to me. My memories of the burrows were as vivid and real as anything I'd experienced in my waking life. I even grew nervous walking around corners, as if White Blade might be waiting to attack. Logically, I knew the writing on my face had little to do with my dreams. It wasn't hard to guess who the real culprits were, and the Steves' laughter when they saw Dickie and me only confirmed my suspicions. Still, I couldn't shake the sense that it was more than coincidence. My dreams didn't feel like dreams anymore. They were spilling out. Taking over.

Dickie and I decided to pretend that we'd marked ourselves. We didn't want to risk having the administration get involved. Fortunately, no one made a big deal about the marks—at least not until last period rolled around and I had to go to Mr. Funt's English class.

Since his divorce, Mr. Funt had become a bit too focused on school. A balding, unpublished writer with a ponytail, he hung around campus for long hours after classes ended, grading papers, drinking coffee, and sponsoring every club that crossed his desk. He was a good teacher—smarter than most of the adults at ASMA. While a lot of teachers resorted to bragging about their advanced degrees and hiding behind their grade books, Mr. Funt treated us as equals. When we discussed stories, he could always point out a few things no one else had noticed, yet he never acted like he knew everything. If you said something interesting, he'd wrinkle his forehead and say, "That's interesting," and sound like he meant it. Overall, I liked Mr. Funt, but he had an annoying habit of reading too much into things.

He stopped me and read my forehead when I came into class. "Hmm . . ." he said. "I don't find that funny."

"Oh, well," I replied. "There's no accounting for taste."

A few students snickered. By this time, my various EAT ME explanations had spread throughout the school.

Mr. Funt frowned and started class. I thought that was it, but later on, while everyone was working on the creative writing assignment he'd given us, he asked me to step outside. The room grew quiet as I stuffed my things into my backpack.

"James," he said, after closing the classroom door, "I think you should see the counselor."

"Why?"

"That"—he gestured to my forehead—"is very distracting. I can't help but wonder what your true intentions were."

"It's nothing," I said.

"No. It is definitely not 'nothing.' I take this sort of thing very seriously. I'd like you to talk with the counselor."

"Is this optional?" I asked.

"Everything's optional. But I plan on stopping by Chuck's office later to make sure you showed up. Understand?"

"Yeah, I understand. I'm in trouble, even though I haven't broken any rules." I scowled. "Why don't you just give me a detention?"

"You're not in trouble, James." Mr. Funt brushed his hand over the strands of side hair that formed his scraggly ponytail. The ends of his fingers were tinted yellow from smoking. "I'm asking you to go because I'm concerned about you."

"Right," I replied. "You got me. This is clearly a cry for help. I woke up this morning and wrote EAT ME on my forehead because I'm thinking of killing myself. Thank God you noticed."

"I don't know why you did it, but you shouldn't expect me to pretend that it's nothing," Mr. Funt said. "Besides, that isn't the only reason I want you to go."

"This is stupid."

"Humor me."

"Fine." I slung my backpack over my shoulder and walked away. I guess I should have been happy to have gotten out of class, but it bothered me that Mr. Funt thought I needed to see a shrink. Just because I'd done a few strange things lately didn't mean I was crazy. It was the people who tried to seem normal all the time who were really messed up.

I got so worked up thinking about how Mr. Funt had singled me out that by the time I reached the hall where Chuck's office was located, I was sweating. The administration had recently turned on the heat for the winter, and they kept it several degrees too high.

I walked past the door to Chuck's office, trying to gather my thoughts before going in. My only experience with Chuck had been at the beginning of the semester, when he'd come to our wing and done the trust fall, but I'd seen him around campus since then. He'd learned every student's name in the first few weeks of school, and whenever he saw someone, he'd say, "How are you doing, _____?" pronouncing the person's name real loud as if to prove that he knew it. Then he'd stop and stare at the person, like he really wanted to hear how they were doing. That was the freaky part, because of his one eye. The thought of him asking me questions and staring at me with his empty socket made me want to hork.

I considered ditching and heading back to my dorm to take a nap, but then Mr. Funt might have Chuck do an emergency intervention or something. Nope. The only way out of this was to stay calm.

After waiting for the hall to clear of other students, I walked back to the door for Health and Student Services and pushed it open. Linda, the secretary, sat at her desk, shuffling papers. Behind her loomed the door to Chuck's room and the door to the nurse. A radio on Linda's bookshelf droned light rock. The muffled sounds of someone talking leaked through Chuck's door. Linda probably kept the radio on to drown out the counseling sessions.

"Hey, Linda." I leaned against the post near her desk, attempting to play it cool. "How's it going?"

"Busy."

"I like your earrings," I said. It was the sort of thing Dickie would say.

Linda touched her earrings to remind herself what she was wearing. The dangly clumps of bright beads clashed with her necklace and striped shirt.

"They're bold," I added. "They go well with your necklace."

"Thank you."

"Amber's my favorite stone. If you can call it a stone, since it's not really, is it?"

"I think it's tree sap," she said.

"Okay. So amber's my favorite tree sap."

She chuckled and shook her head. "What can I help you with?"

"Nothing. Just wanted to say hello. Oh, and I'm supposed to see Chuck."

"Really?"

"Yup." I leaned forward and pulled my hair back to give her a good look.

"Oh, my," she said, reading my forehead. She slid out a sheet from her files and frowned at it. "I'm not sure what category to put that under."

"It's not meant to be an insult. One of my friends snuck into my room and elfed me."

"Elfed you?"

"Wrote on my face while I slept," I explained. "Like elves do mischief in the night."

"You kids," she said. "You're so funny."

"Mr. Funt didn't think it was funny. That's why he sent me here."

"Well, Mr. Funt . . . he's dealing with a lot right now," she said, wrinkling her nose.

"Yeah. His divorce."

We both nodded.

"It's not our policy to force students to talk with a counselor," Linda said. "So is there anything you'd *like* to talk with Chuck about?"

"Nope. I'm feeling pretty sane today. In fact, I'm the sanest person I know, appearances aside."

"I try not to judge by appearances."

"Then is it okay if I leave?"

She shrugged. "I don't see why not. But if ever you *do* need to talk with someone . . ."

"Linda," I said, "I always want to talk with you."

"You're such a charmer."

"Oh." I turned back, as if I'd just remembered something. "If Mr. Funt stops by, will you tell him I was here?"

"No problem."

"Great. Don't work too hard."

I headed for the exit. So far, so good. No one had seen me here, and Linda would cover for me. I was about to make a clean getaway when the door opened and I ran into the Ice Queen. She sidestepped, trying to get around me, only I stepped in the same direction and we collided, chest to chest. It would have been comical if it wasn't so embarrassing.

"Excuse me," she said, sounding annoyed. "I need to get a Band-Aid."

"Sure," I replied. My face burned, and my stomach did flips. All the cool drained out of me.

The Ice Queen gave me a strange look. I had this overwhelming desire to impress her, while at the same time I wanted to ignore her because she couldn't care less about me. And beneath all that, there was something else—a sense of déjà vu that kept me frozen in place. We'd stood this way, blocking each other, before.

"Forget it," she said, turning. A wisp of her blond hair fell across her blue eyes. She hurried off, keeping her head down, the way movie stars do when they want to avoid being photographed.

I tried to tell her to wait, but no words came out. It suddenly hit me why the situation seemed familiar. It had happened last night.

The Thief in my dreams was Ellie.

Part III

O God! I could be bounded in a nutshell,

and count myself a king of infinite space,

were it not that I have bad dreams.

—*HAMLET*, ACT 2, SCENE 2

Winter

THE COLD CAME QUICKLY. Leaves fell from the trees until the branches stood black as cracks against the sky. Winter at ASMA was a lonely, exposed affair. The nearby cornfields were all cut down, leaving nothing but frozen mud and dead stalks, while overhead the pale sky loomed oppressively large, with no hills or leaves to challenge its emptiness. Winds swept through campus, blowing icy snow and dust into muddy drifts against the dorms. Nothing about it looked pretty.

The worst part was that daylight practically disappeared. By December, it was dark at seven in the morning when I first shuffled to school for breakfast, and dark at four in the afternoon when I got out of my last class and headed back to my room. The lack of windows in the main building meant I pretty much went for weeks without seeing the sun.

Everything blended together. The dark of the day merged into the dark of my dreams. Asleep, I wandered the city, not daring to descend into the burrows again since I feared losing control. But after a few weeks of binding demons, the surface streets stood empty. There were only the Nomanchulators, watching hungrily from the shadows, filling the silence with their deadening buzz.

To pass the time, I swigged cough syrup. It wasn't a great high, but it tweaked things enough so I could get through the dreary winter days without driving myself insane. And when the dreariness became too much and the deadening buzz of the Nomanchulators started to creep up on me, I'd cut myself. The bright hot pain always drove the deadness away.

Dickie and I got the Steves back for elfing us by breaking into their room and attaching a car battery to their toilet—one terminal to the water and one to some copper threads we'd taped across the floor. The Steves were such slobs, all we had to do was shove the battery behind the toilet and throw a towel over it to make things look normal. Dickie tried to persuade me to test it out, but having grown up in the sticks, I knew what happened when you peed on an electric fence. The basic mechanics of this were the same.

We hid in the stairwell near their room so we could listen to the fruits of our labor. When Steve Lacone returned from basketball practice, he went to take a leak and *ZING!*—twelve muscle-freezing volts coursed up the stream, causing his voice to shoot through the roof in an unprecedented falsetto. The best part, though, was that Steve Dennon didn't believe anything had actually happened, so he used the toilet right afterward and got zapped, too. Dickie and I nearly gave ourselves hernias holding in our laughter while the Steves cursed about their shocked wankers.

Other than the pranks, I broke up the winter dullness by messing around with Jess. We'd skip class and sneak into dorm rooms or custodians' closets and maul each other. Rumors spread about how we'd done it in the RC's office or on the roof of the school. Although most of the rumors weren't true, neither Jess nor I did much to contradict them. The stories fit my image. Still, no matter how intense things got with Jess, I couldn't keep my mind from wandering. The more wild my life became, the less I felt like I was living it.

Jess must have sensed my distance. "Earth to James," she said one night when we were in the laundry room together. "What's wrong?"

I shrugged. "I'm sick of winter."

She pursed her lips and studied my face. A few times, she'd asked me what I thought of Sage or Sunny. I think she suspected that I might be into someone else. Of course I denied it. If Jess left me, I'd be worse than alone. I'd be no one again.

"I got you something," she said.

"A present?"

"Uh-huh."

"Why?"

"Thought you might need a pick-me-up." Jess reached into her coat pocket and pulled out a silver flask with a red bow tied around it. "Surprise!"

I held the cool metal in my palm. "I can't believe you bought this for me."

"Don't get too excited—I stole it from my old man when I went home last weekend. But I did fill it."

I unscrewed the cap and flinched at the sharp smell of whiskey. "To winter," I said, and took a swig. The whiskey burned a trail to my stomach. It sure beat cough syrup.

Jess and I passed the flask back and forth until it was almost half gone. She grew giddy and threw her arms around my neck, kissing me.

I tried to match her passion, but images of Ellie kept popping up in my head. It wasn't like I was imagining kissing her. Instead, I saw her standing in the doorway with a disapproving look on her face. It annoyed me that I kept thinking of Ellie. I didn't even like her. Granted, she was pretty, but she acted like a cold, elitist snob—exactly the sort of person I couldn't stand. Why she, of all people, appeared in my dreams was beyond me.

Jess pulled back. "What are you thinking about?" she asked.

"Nothing," I lied.

She smirked and bit my shoulder. Then she slipped her hands under my shirt and dragged her nails across my back.

We kept messing around until curfew.

When I returned to my room that night and took my shirt off to go to bed, Dickie freaked. "Jesus," he said, "were you whipped?"

"What?"

"Your back, man," he said. "Look at it."

I craned my neck to see my back in the mirror. Rows of red marks rose out of my flesh from where Jess had scratched me. "Funny," I said. "I didn't feel a thing."

Zero

ghost44: Boo!

johnnyrotten: Hey. I didn't expect to find you logged on.

ghost44: Thought I'd say good morning.

johnnyrotten: It's 11:58 at night.

ghost44: And in a few minutes it'll be morning—the start of a new day. So why are you still at a computer?

johnnyrotten: History assignment. I'm writing a report on the difference between Napoleonic and modern warfare, due in eight hours. You?

ghost44: I'm looking for lost souls to haunt.

johnnyrotten: Find any?

ghost44: Only one, and he's a little peculiar.

johnnyrotten: What makes you say that?

ghost44: I don't know, Mr. Eat Me, Drink Me.

johnnyrotten: That's finally starting to fade, thank you very much. Are you still pissed at me?

ghost44: You mean am I jealous about you sleeping with Jess, the wonder girl?

johnnyrotten: I guess.

ghost44: Relax, cowboy. Ghosts are beyond such petty emotions. Like I said before, we can tell each other anything.

johnnyrotten: I was afraid you weren't going to write me again.

ghost44: No such luck. So how are things with Jess?

johnnyrotten: Complicated.

ghost44: Really?

johnnyrotten: You sure you want us to tell each other anything?

ghost44: Out with it.

johnnyrotten: The thing is, there's this girl that I can't stop thinking about. I mean, I'm obsessed, but I don't like her, and I'm pretty sure she hates me.

ghost44: You're not talking about Jessica Keen, are you?

johnnyrotten: No. That's why things are complicated.

ghost44: Are you going to break up with Jess?

johnnyrotten: So I could ask out a girl who hates me?

ghost44: That's not the point.

johnnyrotten: Then what is?

ghost44: The point is, you should break up with Jess.

johnnyrotten: Why?

ghost44: Uh . . . you're not into her.

johnnyrotten: It's not that simple. I'd be stupid to break up with Jess. She's cute, and wild, and fun. I should like her.

ghost44: Should?

johnnyrotten: Anyway, Jess and I aren't even "going out." We don't exactly call each other boyfriend and girlfriend.

ghost44: Oh, please. I see you two together all the time. You're going out, and that's what's sad.

johnnyrotten: Why's that sad?

ghost44: Because. She's not the right girl for you.

johnnyrotten: Then who is the right girl? You?

ghost44: You can't date the dead, James. Besides, did you ever stop to consider that I might already be going out with someone?

johnnyrotten: Are you?

ghost44: Not really.

johnnyrotten: But you like someone?

ghost44: Maybe.

johnnyrotten: Who?

ghost44: It doesn't matter. I'll never be with him.

johnnyrotten: Why not?

ghost44: Because I can't be with him.

johnnyrotten: ?

ghost44: Look, I used to believe that if only I got the right guy to like me, everything would be okay. I'd feel whole again. And then I'd stop fading away.

johnnyrotten: And you don't believe that now?

ghost44: Nope. Now I know better.

johnnyrotten: Meaning what, exactly?

ghost44: Meaning I know things won't work out, and then I'll lose the only hope I have left. I'd rather be alone than do that.

johnnyrotten: How do you know that's what will happen?

ghost44: Because that's what always happens.

johnnyrotten: It doesn't have to be that way. It might be different this time.

ghost44: Trust me. It wouldn't be.

johnnyrotten: But it could.

ghost44: Not for me. It's simple math—anything times zero is zero.

johnnyrotten: You're not a zero.

ghost44: The funny thing is I keep trying to be.

johnnyrotten: Huh?

ghost44: Good night, James.

johnnyrotten: That's it? You're not going to explain?

ghost44: Sorry. Even ghosts need to sleep.

HγPoThєRmia

JESS CALLED ON FRIDAY NIGHT to coax me over to
her dorm to "study." Finals started the next week and
everyone was frantic about preparing for exams. I could
have used a break, but the prospect of spending another
hour in a laundry room making out with Jess made me
anxious. I figured I needed to be alone to get my head
straightened out, so I told Jess that I had to meet with my
chemistry group.

"It's Friday," Jess said. "You can study tomorrow."

"I'm supposed to meet them tonight," I lied. "One of
my lab partners is going home for the weekend, and we
need to trade results."

Jess paused. "That bites," she finally said.

When social hour arrived, I threw on my coat and
headed out to walk the pond and sip some whiskey. I

didn't worry too much about Jess catching me. The campus looked empty. Because of finals, and because of the cold, almost no one else was outside. Pausing beneath the willow tree, I threw back a swig.

"Nice night," someone said.

I scrambled to hide the flask. The person had been standing so still by the tree's trunk that I hadn't seen her. When she moved, I recognized her slender silhouette.

"You can see a lot of stars tonight," the Ice Queen said.

I looked at the sky, then back at her, confused. "What are you doing here?"

"I'm walking," she said.

"Alone?"

"Don't sound so surprised."

I glanced at my dorm, but I didn't want to head in yet and it would have been awkward to walk away from her. "Can I walk with you?"

"You don't have to. I can handle being alone."

"I want to," I said. Then I realized how desperate I probably sounded. "I mean, I was going to anyway. That's why I came out here—to walk around the pond. Here." I got out the flask. "Want some?"

Ellie took the flask and sniffed it warily.

"It'll warm you up," I added, trying to sound suave, only as soon as I said it, I wished I hadn't. It was such a sleazy line. She probably thought I wanted to get her drunk so I could bust a move. "Forget it," I muttered, reaching to take the flask back. "Don't let me corrupt you."

She glanced at me and drank a swig before passing it back.

We followed the path around the pond, walking in silence. After all the time I'd spent obsessing over her, you'd think I could have come up with something interesting to say. But nope. *Nada.* My brain stayed blank as snow. I threw down another swig, then Ellie took the flask and drank without wiping the top.

"Do you have many finals?" I asked, even though it was the dumbest, most cliché question in the book.

"Mostly papers," she said. "And the physics exam on Monday."

"Sorry. Lame question. I don't really care about finals."

"Oh."

"I mean, good luck on the physics exam."

Ellie grinned. "Thanks, I think."

I clenched my jaw and glanced away. We were almost to the far end of the pond, near where Sage Fisher's dad had thrown the picnic. I thought of how I'd tried to introduce myself to Ellie after that, and how she'd ignored me and said she wasn't impressed. That's how I always felt around her—unimpressive.

The silence between us thickened. In another few minutes we'd be by the dorms again, and then we'd go our separate ways and she'd always think I was this quiet nobody.

I took a drink. The whiskey made my head light and warm. "What was it like?" I asked, looking at the pond.

"What was what like?"

"The Mark Watson triathlon. You know, having him run out here, and swim the pond and punch out some guy."

She smirked. "Embarrassing."

"But he did it for you."

"Trust me: that's not the way to win a girl's heart." Ellie kicked a frozen dirt clod. It slid along some thin ice near the edge of the pond, then plunked into the open water in the middle.

"Did you like him?" I asked.

"Who?"

"Mark Watson."

"We only went out for two weeks before he got expelled," she said. "I didn't get to know him very well, but he was funny. He made me feel special."

I pictured Mark Watson—tall, athletic, golden-haired—swimming madly across the pond toward Ellie. He could have run around the pond, but he didn't.

"I'd swim it," I said.

"What?"

"I'm just saying, it's not like Mark Watson was that special. I'd swim the pond right now."

"It's frozen."

"Just around the edges," I said. "Dare me to go swimming?"

"No."

"Why not?"

Ellie looked at me, perplexed. "Because it's too cold. No one would go swimming now."

"I would."

"Whatever."

"I'm serious," I said. "Cold water doesn't bother me. I'm like a dolphin. I can lower my heart rate and control my breathing so it doesn't feel cold."

Ellie scoffed.

"I'll prove it," I said, throwing off my jacket. Goose bumps prickled my arms.

"Don't be stupid."

"You should try it." I kicked off my shoes and socks. My bare feet snapped through the ice around the edge. "It feels good."

"Quit joking."

"I'm not joking. Dare me?"

"No." Ellie started to walk away. Her legs seemed fragile and childish in her heavy winter boots.

"Come on, dare me."

She didn't stop. I had to do something to get her attention—something no one else would do—so I pulled off my shirt and jumped in.

Lightning flashes filled my head as soon as I hit the water. All I could manage was to dunk myself once and clamber out. My skin stung from the cold as I hopped around in my wet jeans to shake the water off.

"Hey!" I called, but Ellie kept walking.

I tried shouting her name, only my teeth were chattering too much. She didn't even look back to see if I was okay. I couldn't believe she was still ignoring me.

My jaw shivered uncontrollably and my hands weren't working very well as I struggled to pull on my socks and shoes. Then my chest and arms started to shake. The shivers grew worse, becoming whole-body convulsions.

By the time I managed to get my second shoe on, the convulsions passed, leaving me pleasantly tired. I didn't feel cold anymore. Sitting shirtless on the snow, I gazed across the pond. Ellie had gone inside, and I couldn't see anyone else out. Not a single person. A few snowflakes glistened in the orange lights of the dorms, while stars shimmered in the crisp black sky.

The dorms looked far away and flat, like a painting of a campus. I wanted to be part of it—to be inside among the people, laughing in the warm light—but it seemed too distant and unreal.

After a while, my eyelids grew heavy. I lay on my coat and looked at the stars, thinking about how they were so far away they could have vanished a thousand years before their light ever reached us.

Numb

THE THIEF LEANED OVER ME, *beautiful against the winter sky. "Wake up, James," she said. "You have to wake up!"*

But I didn't want to wake. Sleep pulled at me, as if I were sinking into honey. I wanted to drown in my dreams.

Later, someone shined a light in my eyes. I squinted into the brightness. Two figures knelt beside me where the Thief had been.

At first, I thought it was Nick and Kiana. They both wore dark uniforms, and their faces looked pale. The woman had her hand on my neck. "Careful not to jolt him," she said.

One of them kept shining a flashlight in my face. I tried to tell him to quit it and let me sleep, but I couldn't get my jaw to move. My mouth tasted terrible—stale whiskey and stomach acid. Walkie-talkies beeped, filling the silence with staticky chatter while the two figures slid me onto a stretcher and placed something heavy on my chest.

The sting of it woke me up.

Whatever they'd put on me burned like crazy. I pushed it away, but they strapped me down and put it on me again. My skin felt as if it were blistering off my body.

"Relax," the woman said. "The blanket's not hot. It's barely even warm."

My eyes focused on her uniform, illuminated by the red and blue flash of ambulance lights. It sounded as if a crowd of people had gathered nearby, but I couldn't look because my head was fixed into a foam-rubber block.

They lifted me and carried me across the field toward the square, where the ambulance waited. I was like a baby—all swaddled up and ready to be carted somewhere. It was beyond embarrassing.

At the hospital, the doctor said I had hypothermia. I tried to explain that I was just tired and needed to sleep, but they wouldn't leave me alone. They put a mask over my mouth with a hose connected to this machine that made the air warm and humid. Then they drew some blood and stuck a hot IV into my veins, so it wasn't just my skin that burned. Every joint in my body ached. After a while, the convulsions started again, causing my teeth to chatter uncontrollably.

A nurse kept checking my temperature and fiddling with the dials on the blanket and hot-air thingy. Every time it stopped burning, she'd turn it up a notch and the hurt would come back.

Apparently, they had to be careful that I didn't warm too quickly. During one of her visits, the nurse told me this story about these sailors who'd been shipwrecked in the Arctic and were left floating in icy water for almost forty minutes before a boat came and rescued them. Everyone thought it was a miracle that they were alive. Then the captain had them go down to the hold to drink some hot coffee so they could warm up, and ten minutes later all the rescued sailors died—something to do with shock and a low core body temperature.

"The only thing worse than hypothermia and caffeine is hypothermia and alcohol." The nurse smirked at me, and I knew I was busted.

My parents arrived at the hospital a little while later. Moms hovered about my bed, tucking the blanket in and feeling my forehead with the back of her hand, as if she had some supermom ability to tell my exact temperature by touch.

"My poor baby," she said. "What were you thinking?"

She acted especially concerned when the doctor came to check on me. "Are you sure he's going to be okay?" she asked for the third or fourth time.

The doctor, a thirtysomething, surprisingly tall man, stifled a yawn. "Hypothermia is very treatable."

"But what if no one had found him?"

"Things might have been more difficult then," the doctor said. "However, the human body can come back from extreme cold, given proper treatment. There've even been cases where hypothermia victims were thought DOA, only to regain consciousness in the morgue. No one's dead until they're warm and dead." He patted my shoulder, as if this thought should comfort me.

"Doctor, thank you for saving my boy," Moms said.

The doctor cleared his throat and fidgeted with his clipboard. Dad stood off to the side, hands in his pockets, jangling change.

I lay between them, wishing this whole ridiculous exchange would take place without me. Moms was acting like a character in a soap opera, but I knew if I questioned her about it, she'd roll her eyes and say I wouldn't know politeness if it bit me.

The doctor checked his beeper. "I'm afraid there's another patient I have to see." He patted my shoulder again. "The next time you want to swim, son, wait for summer. Okay?"

"Okay," I said, even though his condescending manner pissed me off.

Moms started in on me again after that. "Did you hear what the doctor said? You could have frozen to death. Honestly, James, what were you thinking? If your girlfriend hadn't called security . . ."

"Who?"

"The girl that found you." Moms looked to my dad for help remembering her name. "Ella? Ellen?"

"Ellie," I said. "And she's not my girlfriend."

"She's very nice," Moms replied, glancing from me to my dad. "Wasn't she nice?"

"Very nice," Dad said.

I was too tired to tell them how wrong they were.

The nurses didn't waste any time shooing me out once I got back to a normal temperature. It was two in the morning, but they didn't seem to care. To them, I guess it was just another workday. The halls bustled with people, and the hospital lights were as bright as ever.

I had to wear some flimsy mint-green hospital scrubs home since my pants were wet and the paramedics hadn't thought to grab the jacket or T-shirt I'd left by the pond. My dad signed the discharge papers while Moms busied herself talking with Hassert in the waiting room—just my luck that he'd been on duty. I guess he'd accompanied my parents to the hospital. He nodded at something Moms said, looking very serious.

"Your parents are going to drive you home," he said to me. "The administration will meet tomorrow to discuss what's best for you." He gave Moms a concerned RC look and added, "I'll do what I can."

I nearly choked. Without a doubt, Hassert would do what he could to get me expelled. He'd probably already gotten a copy of my blood alcohol level to use as evidence against me.

"We'll call you once a decision has been reached," he said to Moms.

She thanked him for all his kindness. Fortunately, Dad led me out before I lost it.

Dad had stayed pretty quiet at the hospital, but on the drive back, he droned on and on about medical bills, making sure I knew how much everything had cost. "Eight hundred dollars for the ambulance. A hundred and twenty dollars in blood tests. Probably over a thousand for the hospital care. They really gouge you," he said. Never mind that insurance would cover most of it. "That's one expensive drink," Dad joked.

Moms scowled at him and said it wasn't funny.

After that, Dad didn't say anything. He turned onto the highway, and the road began to hum beneath us. I rested my head against the car door, pretending to sleep for most of the ride home. The cool ridge of the door edge creased my cheek. Despite all the pain of warming up—the burning and aching—I still felt numb. I pushed my thumbnail into the tips of my fingers and pinched the soft skin on the underside of my arms. It hurt, but only vaguely, as if I hadn't come all the way back. "Deadened." That's what the doctor had said. "Some nerves might be deadened."

SuSPeNSion

PRINCIPAL DURN CALLED MY PARENTS the next day to inform them that I was suspended for the rest of the semester, which was only five days. I listened in from the phone in my bedroom. The administration saw the incident as my third strike, after the cafeteria stunt and the "profanity" I'd scrawled on my forehead. According to Principal Durn, I was lucky not to be expelled. As he put it, I now "hung by a thread," with "my continued enrollment being contingent upon my academic performance." In other words, if I didn't ace my finals, I'd get the boot.

My suspension spanned finals week, so I had to arrange for alternate times to take my exams. Ironically, this meant that my study-break swim had actually earned me an extra week to prepare.

The administration agreed to let me drop by campus on Monday to turn in assignments and pick up my books. Hassert assigned a security guard to accompany me. He made it very clear that I couldn't talk with any students while I went around arranging things with the teachers. People stared at me like they were seeing a condemned man walking to the gallows.

I passed Dickie in the commons. "You're coming back, right?" he called, ignoring the security guard's glare.

"Who knows?" I said, trying to sound stoic. "Depends if I'm good."

At home, I was trapped. I didn't have a car, and there wasn't anything to do in my town. There wasn't even anyone to talk to. I tried calling Jess, but she didn't respond to my messages, and whenever I checked online for ghost44, she wasn't logged on.

My parents pestered me constantly about staying in my room all day. Anytime Moms asked me to go shopping with her, or Dad called for me to give him a hand with something in the basement, I shouted back that I needed to study and they left me alone. I actually did try to study, too, but I could barely get my eyes to focus on my books. Instead, I slept.

With the curtains closed and the door jammed shut by a chair, I managed to take two or three naps a day. My dreams seemed more interesting and real than anything going on in my normal life. Awake, I was clumsy and sluggish and barely able to find a reason to get out of bed, but when I dreamed, I could move quick as thought. I even learned to fly.

The first time I attempted it, I was terrified. The guides convinced me to step off a building, and immediately I began to fall so fast that the air whistled past my ears. Then I closed my eyes and focused on bending things, the way Nick had told me to do, so instead of falling down, I'd fall out. That's the secret to flight—it's falling in a different direction. I couldn't go as fast or as high as I wanted to, but the rush of air around me as I swooped between buildings felt incredible.

Flying helped me to find more demons. Most were weak, mangy ones that I had little trouble binding. Some were even ones I'd fought before. Nick explained that as long as one demon was free, others would get loose.

I spent hours soaring over the deserted streets, perfecting my skills on the strays I spotted. The more time I spent in the city, the stronger I became.

Kiana commented on the shift after a few nights. "You're more here now," she said, squeezing my arm. "You're more focused and in control. You can win this war if . . ." Her voice trailed off.

"If what?" I asked.

"You know what has to be done," Nick said. "You can't hide here forever."

I thought of White Blade. I hadn't descended into the burrows since the night he'd beaten me. The guides seemed to know that I'd needed to build my confidence back up. Now, though, Nick acted agitated, like he thought I was wasting time.

"I'm starting to wonder if we backed the wrong horse," he said.

"Don't listen to him." Kiana bumped her hip playfully against mine. "You won't let us down. I'm sure of it."

MaNneQUiN

AFTER FIVE DAYS OF SLEEPING most of the time, I finally agreed to go shopping with Moms.

"It's not supposed to be a punishment," she said. "Even if you are suspended. Honestly, James, you need new clothes." She looked at my faded jeans and torn T-shirt with disgust. My favorite black sport coat had gotten a little ragged around the cuffs from being worn so much. "Honey, the hobo style isn't *in* anymore."

"It never was in," I said. "That's the point."

"Don't you want new clothes for Christmas?"

I paused. It wasn't that I didn't want new clothes. It was that going shopping with Moms never ended up the way I thought it would.

"If you don't go shopping with me, I'll buy things for you that you don't like," she threatened.

I thought of the pile of bright-colored polo shirts I had in my closet from previous Christmases. "Okay," I said. "But I'm not getting any shirts with collars. Collars freak me out."

Moms rolled her eyes and grabbed her purse.

When we got to the mall, she made a beeline for her favorite department store. I've always been a bit confused about where I fit in department stores. I mean, there's the boys' area, with the Underoos and cartoons and stuff, and the men's area, with all the three-piece suits and shiny shoes. In between are these weird subgroups, like the sweatpants and sports teams area, or the trying-too-hard-to-be-hip jeans area, or the preppy sweater and polo shirt area. According to department stores, boys are supposed to progress naturally from Underoos, to sweatpants, to jeans, to preppy clothes, to suits. I wanted to mix it up, taking a sport coat from men's, jeans from the teen area, and a T-shirt with G.I. Joe on it from the kids' area, only they probably didn't have any big enough to fit me.

Moms went straight to the preppy area.

"Hey," she said, picking out a dark blue V-neck sweater, "try this on."

"No way," I replied. "I'm not in the yacht club."

"Honey, this is what guys are wearing."

"How do you know what guys are wearing?"

"I have a sense," she said. "Just put it on."

I slipped off my coat and pulled the sweater over my head, keeping my back to her so she wouldn't see the cuts on my arm I'd recently given myself with a compass point. Then I turned and slouched, trying to make the sweater look as bad as possible.

"That's nice," she said.

A salesman wandered over—a young guy in a white button-down shirt, blue power tie, and hair so perfectly gelled he looked like a Ken doll.

"Is there anything I can help you with?" Ken offered.

"What do you think?" Moms said to the salesguy. "Does that look good on him?"

The guy cocked his head and stared. I slouched a little more, pulling one arm in while letting the other hang low, like the Hunchback of Notre Dame.

"Stand up, honey," Moms said.

"Very sharp," the salesguy crooned. "The fit creates clean lines, and the color pulls out his eyes."

Moms smiled, pleased to have found an ally.

"Pulls out my eyes?" I said, picturing the sweater attempting to gouge my eyes out. Moms and the salesguy gave me odd looks, like *I* was the weird one.

"I don't know." Moms fiddled with the sweater. "The dark blue washes him out, but the cut is good."

"We have it in maroon," Ken doll said. "It's very chic. I bought a maroon one myself the day they came out."

"I hate maroon," I said.

"Don't be so picky," Moms chided. "Maroon is in."

Ken burbled something into a walkie-talkie, and a

moment later a girl in high heels, white shirt, and short checkered skirt approached. She was cute, with streaked blond hair and a perky figure. At first I thought she must be in college, but as she got closer, I realized she was probably around my age, except she dressed older. Not many girls at ASMA wore high heels.

The two salespeople talked, then the girl went off to find the sweater.

"We have slacks that will go nicely, too," Ken said.

"Wonderful," Moms agreed. "You need new slacks, don't you?"

"No."

Moms browsed through a rack of "slacks" with Ken, as if I hadn't said anything. I looked at the nearby mannequins with their blank, angular faces and nonexistent mouths. For some reason, I could never be myself around Moms. At school, I knew how to act, but now this silence lodged in my throat and I felt myself getting pulled back into who I'd been before—an anonymous plastic blob for her to pose and dress up.

The cute girl returned with three different sweaters to try on, and Ken held out some slacks. "First let's fit you into these," he said. "So we can see if the colors work."

He and Moms led me to the dressing room, while the cute girl followed. I had to put on the "slacks." Even though I wanted to make them look crappy, I couldn't do it in front of the girl.

"Very chic," Ken said.

"So what's the difference between slacks and pants?" I asked. "And what about trousers? Do you have any *trousers* here?"

The salesgirl smiled.

"Lift up the shirt and turn around," Moms said.

I scowled and turned.

"The butt is everything," she said to the salesgirl. "Men's pants have to show off the butt. Don't they?"

"*Mom . . .*" I protested.

"Come on, James. You know it's true."

"*You're* his mother?" the salesgirl replied.

"That's what they tell me."

"I thought you were, like, his older sister. Your top is so cute."

"No way. I was admiring yours," Moms replied, sounding like a teenager. She had about sixteen different personalities, depending on who she was with—that's why I called her Moms.

"Wow. I could trade clothes with you," the salesgirl said. "I'd never trade clothes with my own mom."

Moms beamed. They were all on her side now. She leaned over and whispered something to the salesgirl, and the salesgirl giggled and whispered something back.

I stood with my hands in my pockets. "So do I keep turning?"

"The slacks are good, right?" Moms asked the salesgirl.

"Definitely. Smooth-fronted dress slacks on guys are way cool."

Moms cocked her head and stared at me as if she were a big-time fashion director. I wanted to run, or scream, or throw up.

"You need a haircut," she said. "Pull it back from your face to make it short."

I did, praying it would be over soon.

"That's the look," she said.

"Totally," the salesgirl agreed.

I let my hair fall back over my eyes. "I feel like some brainless *GQ* poseur. Like I ought to change my name to Brad and drive a Hummer."

"Don't be weird," Moms said. "It's perfect. We'll take it."

The salesgirl grinned. "You are the coolest mom."

Ken doll rang us up. Everything was expensive, but Moms didn't bat an eye. She liked to pretend we were rich.

"Why don't you wear your new clothes out," she said.

The salesgirl slipped around behind me and clipped the tags. "There. You're a new man."

Moms thanked her and told her to throw my old sport coat and jeans away.

"Don't," I said, reaching for my clothes.

"Honey, *Goodwill* wouldn't even take those things."

"That's because I bought them at *Goodwill*."

"You're such a joker."

"I'm not joking," I snapped.

The salespeople looked at each other, then the girl handed me my clothes.

Once we were out of the store, Moms stopped and faced me. "What's gotten into you?"

"What do you mean?" I asked, angry that she blamed me for messing things up.

"You used to love shopping."

I scoffed, wondering what bizarro-world past she was remembering. "No, I didn't. I never liked shopping."

Her face crumpled. For a moment, I feared she might cry, then her eyes focused on something behind me. "I'm trying, James. I really am," she said. "Can't we be happy? For once, for just a few hours, can't we pretend to have fun and be happy?" There was a note of desperation in her voice, as if her life depended on whether I said yes or no.

"Sure," I replied, swallowing myself. "I'm sorry. I really like the sweater."

RunaWay

I CALLED JESS'S DORM ROOM the next day. It was the last day of finals, and all the students were supposed to pack and go home for winter break after they finished exams. I worried that she might have left already, and I didn't have her cell number.

She picked up after the third ring. "Hey, Jess."

"Oh," she answered. "It's you."

"I think it's me," I said. "I mean, you can never be certain, can you? I don't always feel like myself."

Jess didn't say anything. In the background, I heard Rachel talking with someone else. I realized how strange I must have sounded. Ghost44 would have understood, but I had to be careful with Jess.

"Why'd you call?" she asked.

"I miss you," I said, surprised by how cold she sounded. "I haven't talked with anyone in days. I'm going crazy here."

"Crazy how? Crazy like you're wearing lipstick and talking to your hand, or crazy like you dissed your incredibly awesome girlfriend to go skinny-dipping in a frozen pond?"

"Sorry about the pond thing."

"Save it. I knew there was someone else."

"You mean Ellie?" I wanted to kick myself for not thinking of what Jess might have heard. This explained why she hadn't returned my calls. "You think I snuck out to see the Ice Queen?"

"Why I'm even talking to you is beyond me."

"Hold on. There's nothing going on between me and Ellie."

"Bullshit."

"It's true," I said. "It was a coincidence that she was there."

"Then why'd you go swimming?"

"I was bored. Honestly, Ellie wasn't even around when I jumped in the pond." Technically, it was true, but I didn't know if Jess would buy it.

"I'm not stupid," she replied. "I know Ellie was there. She called security."

"She must have seen me jump." I racked my brain for some way to convince her. "Look, if there was something going on between Ellie and me, why would she just leave me there? Why wouldn't she walk me inside so I could warm up? It's because of her that I got suspended."

Jess didn't say anything for a few seconds. "You could have frozen to death."

"I was fine."

"Yeah, right." She still sounded pissed.

I tried to change the subject. "You ever think about running away?"

No answer.

"I wish we could run away together," I said.

"Where would you want to go?" she finally replied.

"Someplace interesting. California, maybe. Or Seattle. Someplace where no one knows us—so we could start over."

"Why do you want to start over?"

"I don't know," I said. "I just need to get away from here."

"Why? What happened?" she asked, concern breaking through her anger.

"Nothing happened. Nothing ever happens here." Even though it was the truth, it sounded like a diversion. Let her think I'd survived fistfights and abuse, because no one makes a movie about a bored middle-class teenager living in a cornfield with nice parents.

I heard a door shut in the background and the other voices grew distant. Jess must have stepped into the bathroom to talk. "You okay, James?"

"Yeah. I'm great," I said. "I just think running away

would be fun. We could steal a car and drive out west and rob convenience stores like Bonnie and Clyde, or that other movie—*True Romance.*"

"Never saw it."

"It's classic. Anyhow, are you going home for break?"

"Where else would I go?"

"Some people go to Florida for Christmas. Or Paris."

"Nope. Not my family. Going to IHOP is the closest my dad gets to traveling."

"I've got an idea. How about I catch a bus to Chicago and stay with you?"

"At my dad's place?" she replied. "No way, J.T. How about I borrow the car and rescue you?"

I pictured Jess with her tattooed chest, piercings, and combat boots meeting my parents. They'd probably call the cops when she arrived. "That won't work," I said.

"Why not?"

"It's too far."

"I don't care. I'll pick you up and we'll go on a dinner date. We can be normal teenagers."

"That's the last thing in the world I want to be," I said. "Besides, isn't the guy supposed to pick the girl up?"

"You don't have a license."

"I have a learner's permit."

"How's Tuesday sound?"

"Not good."

Jess sighed. "I thought you missed me."

"I do."

"So what's the problem?"

"There's no place to eat here," I said, scrambling for a way to keep her from coming.

"Then we'll have dinner at your house."

"With my parents?"

"I'm good with parents. I can be very sweet when I want to."

"So you're inviting yourself over for dinner?"

"Yup. Then I'm whisking you away and ravishing you."

I tried to come up with some other alternative. "What about running away?"

Jess chuckled. "Maybe after dinner."

Katabasis

ON SATURDAY, AFTER ALL the students had gone home, the administration allowed me to return to ASMA to take my exams. Dad dropped me off. I actually got a little excited about taking exams since it meant I'd get to be back on campus, if only for a few hours. But as soon as I entered the main building, things felt different. Other than some teachers grading papers and a custodian vacuuming the orange carpet, no one was there. The emptiness drove me up the wall. I couldn't stop listening to the tick of the clock or the scratch of my pencil on the page as I wrote out answers.

Most of the teachers gave me the exam and went back to grading, but Mr. Funt wanted to talk. I didn't even have to take an exam with him since the final project was a short story and I'd turned mine in before I'd left. It was a good story, too, about a boy who lived in two worlds. Mr. Funt had said that the only thing a writer needed to be was honest, and this story was the most honest thing I'd ever written. I'd even pulled a few scenes from my dreams.

I figured the story would blow Mr. Funt away. It had more symbolism in it than most of the stories we'd talked about in class and the plot was full of action, so I wasn't all that surprised when I dropped by his office to pick it up and he asked if I could stay a minute.

"I heard about what happened at the pond," Mr. Funt said.

I shrugged, expecting him to cut to the chase and tell me how he realized now, after reading my story, that he'd misjudged me. I wasn't some messed-up kid who needed to see a shrink—I was a literary genius. He'd probably encourage me to publish.

"Do you want to talk about that, James?" he asked.

"Talk about what?"

"Why you keep engaging in these self-destructive behaviors."

I glanced at my arm, but I was wearing my usual sport coat so all my scars were covered. "I'm not trying to destroy myself," I said. "I really like myself."

Mr. Funt rubbed his jaw. His stubble made a sound like sandpaper on rough wood. "The Greeks called it *kata-basis*," he said, "from *kata*, meaning down, and *baimen*, meaning to go. Hence the term refers to a descent to the darkest depths whereby a person may discover who he truly is."

He inhaled loudly through his nose, like he did when he gave a lecture in class. "A few Native American tribes called it ashes time," he continued, "because the young men of the tribe were covered in ashes to remind them of the death of their child selves. Then they were sent into the wilderness with only a blanket, and if they came back before they found their name, the people of their tribe would treat them as ghosts. No one would talk to them. No one would acknowledge them. No one would see them. Some wandered for years looking for their true name. Are you with me?"

I nodded, even though I had no idea what he was getting at.

"Ancient cultures had their rites of passage—their ways of challenging youth to discover an adult self. But what do we do now?" Mr. Funt rubbed his jaw again, seeming to consider his own question. "Standardized tests? Sports? Keg parties?" He shook his head. "In the absence of real challenges, teens must devise ways to transform themselves."

"Sounds better than wandering for years with a blanket," I said.

Mr. Funt gave me a concerned look. "I know you're exploring, James. Testing your limits. Plumbing the depths, trying to discover who you are. But be careful. Descend too far into that darkness and you might not return." He paused, as if this advice should instantly change my life. "You might lose yourself entirely."

"Okay." I fiddled with a button on my coat, wishing he'd just give me my story and let me go.

"Sometimes," he continued, "when things are the worst for us, we don't see that they're bad. It's when we need it the most that we forget how to ask for help."

"Okay," I repeated, getting annoyed.

Mr. Funt raised his arms slightly, as if he wanted to hug. "If you need to talk, I'm here."

I backed away, catching a whiff of stale coffee and cigarettes. I wasn't the one with problems here. It wasn't like I smoked a pack a day and clung to a ponytail even though I was going bald. It wasn't like I was getting a divorce.

"Hey, what are you doing for the holidays?" I asked.

"Not much," Mr. Funt said, returning to his desk. "Grading papers, mostly."

I nodded. "So you're spending it alone?"

"Yes."

"That's too bad," I said. "You know, if *you* need to talk with anyone . . ."

He frowned and shuffled through a stack of papers. "Here you go, James," he said, handing me my story. "I think this is what you came for."

"Thanks, Mr. Funt. You take care of yourself, okay?"

He waved me off, not responding.

I hurried down the hall, feeling a little guilty for how

I'd acted, but his insistence that I needed help pissed me off. He hadn't even said anything about my story.

I sat on the front steps to the school and flipped through the pages to read his comments. There weren't any marks on most of the pages. No stars, or exclamation points, or spelling corrections. Just a grade, B–, scrawled in red ink on the last page, and one line that read: *Come back to earth, James.*

I crumpled the story and threw it away. That's what you get for trying to write something honest.

B\ind

johnnyrotten: Hey! I've been waiting for days, hoping you'd log on.

ghost44: The ice man speaketh.

johnnyrotten: Where've you been?

ghost44: Sick. I think we must be twins. After you jumped in the pond, I became ill. Very ill. But unlike some, I still had to take my finals.

johnnyrotten: Before you turn all Kermit with envy, you should know that I had to take my finals. I just finished them.

ghost44: Congratulations. I'll send you a muffin.

johnnyrotten: Thanks.

ghost44: You doing okay?

johnnyrotten: Please, don't start. I already went through this hug-fest-don't-hate-yourself thing with Mr. Funt.

ghost44: Right, because it's totally idiotic for people to wonder if you're okay.

johnnyrotten: Did I mention that Mr. Funt tried to hug me?

ghost44: People worry about you.

johnnyrotten: Why? Because I don't dress like everyone else? Because I have purple hair? Because I got bored and took a swim?

ghost44: Because people care about you.

johnnyrotten: Shh . . . I hear a *Lifetime* sound track coming on.

ghost44: I'm serious, James. How are you?

johnnyrotten: Let's see. . . . My hands are numb, if that's what you're asking. I think they got frostbit from the pond. It feels like I'm wearing gloves all the time.

ghost44: And?

johnnyrotten: And getting suspended sucked. Winter break is long enough as is—not that I miss school so much. It's just I don't fit in at home anymore. As if I ever fit. It's so claustrophobic here.

ghost44: Tell me about it. My mom knocks on my door five times a day and attempts to shove snickerdoodles and spinach down my throat. I'm like a pig she's fattening for slaughter.

johnnyrotten: Snickerdoodles and spinach?

ghost44: She thinks if I ate some holiday cheer with iron, I'd be great. She even threw a few red peppers into the spinach to make it look more "Christmassy."

johnnyrotten: Yum.

ghost44: So how are the holiday festivities at your house?

johnnyrotten: Jess is driving out to rescue me. The rents will probably freak when they see her.

ghost44: I thought you two were over.

johnnyrotten: I never said that.

ghost44: You said you weren't into her.

johnnyrotten: She's just a friend who wants to save me from my supreme boredom and impending mental breakdown.

ghost44: Does she know she's *just a friend*?

johnnyrotten: She invited herself out. What could I say? It's better than being alone.

ghost44: You're not alone. You've got me.

johnnyrotten: Great—my very own ghost to haunt me.

ghost44: I prefer to think of myself as a brain poltergeist—a mental mischief maker and disturber of thoughts.

johnnyrotten: As nice as that sounds, it's not exactly the same as being with someone.

ghost44: If that's the way you feel, I'll go haunt someone else.

johnnyrotten: Wait! I take it back. I like to be haunted. Really. It's the best thing that's happened to me all week.

ghost44: Better than Jess coming over?

johnnyrotten: That's a tough one. I mean, Jess hasn't come over yet, so I can't exactly compare the two. She's driving out on Tuesday.

ghost44: You are so clueless. That was completely, one hundred percent the wrong answer. Now I have to haunt you.

johnnyrotten: Is this when maggots start squirming out of the chicken I ate or my Curious George doll attacks me?

ghost44: Nope. That sort of thing is the work of far lesser ghosts. Your punishment is that you have to listen to a story.

johnnyrotten: Sounds terrifying.

ghost44: It's a very tragic story.

johnnyrotten: I like tragedies.

ghost44: Figures. Now, pay attention. . . .

ghost44: Once upon a time, there was a little birdie who waited so long to fly south for the winter that when he finally took off, he got caught in an ice storm. He tried to keep flying, but his wings froze and he fell into a field.

johnnyrotten: Splat!

ghost44: Not yet. See, the little birdie was lucky—he landed in a pile of cow poo, which cushioned the impact.

johnnyrotten: Hold on. You said *poo*! That's the dirtiest word I've ever seen you write.

ghost44: You know me: I cuss like a sailor.

johnnyrotten: Poo-poodle-holy-poopies!

ghost44: May I continue the story now?

johnnyrotten: By all means.

ghost44: Well, the cow poo was so fresh, its steamy warmth thawed the little birdie's wings.

johnnyrotten: Hooray for poo!

ghost44: So it would seem. But . . . just as the little birdie started to feel good again, a cat came along, pulled him out, and ate him. Know what the moral is?

johnnyrotten: Cats eat shitty food?

ghost44: There are two, actually. One is that sometimes being in poo isn't such a bad thing. And the other is that sometimes those who get you out of poo aren't your friends.

johnnyrotten: Are you saying Jess might eat me?

ghost44: I'm saying maybe you don't need to be rescued.

Maybe you should be alone right now so you can figure things out.

johnnyrotten: Funny. Mr. Funt said something similar—about descending into darkness.

ghost44: It's only when it's dark out that we can see the stars shine.

johnnyrotten: I'm still waiting for the stars to shine. I feel so blind sometimes.

ghost44: That's because you are.

johnnyrotten: What do you mean?

ghost44: I don't know, James. Sometimes I think I must be blind too.

Ashes Time

I FELL ASLEEP THINKING ABOUT what ghost44 and Mr. Funt had said—about katabasis, and darkness, and finding my true name. When I woke in the city, I headed for the elevator with renewed determination.

"About time you got back on the horse," Nick said once I made it to the burrows.

Kiana helped me to my feet and adjusted the scarf that covered my face. The nightclub stood empty. A deafening buzz filled the air, punctuated by the clash of metal against metal.

"The battle's already started," Nick explained, leading us up a fire escape to the roof. "It's time you choose a side."

Nomanchulators, too numerous to count, filled the space between buildings. Their chittering had grown so loud it made my head numb. In their midst, fighting off their attacks, stood White Blade.

At first I thought the Nomanchulators would overwhelm him, but he used the narrow alley to his advantage, keeping them from surrounding him while he cut through their numbers. I watched from the roof, amazed. Even though White Blade was my enemy, I found myself hoping he'd beat back the deadening swarm.

"Now's your chance," Nick said. "Bind him while he's distracted."

"But he's fighting them," I replied. "Isn't that a good thing?"

"If he defeats them, he'll become stronger."

"Think about it, J.T.," Kiana added. "Once he kills the Nomanchulators, what will he do to you?"

I felt my jaw, remembering how quickly White Blade had beaten me before. Next time, I might not be lucky enough to escape. "He's not like the others, is he?" I asked.

"He's a criminal," Nick said.

"But not a demon?"

"Not exactly."

I looked at Nick, but he didn't say anything more. Kiana put her hand on my arm. "Only one of you can survive. You have to bind him."

"And if I can't?"

"You have to," she repeated. "It's the only way to win."

White Blade cut through the swarm, pushing toward the Nomanchulator leader—a creature who stood twice as tall as the others, with spidery limbs and a grotesque mosquito mouth. Silver cable glinted at White Blade's side. Tools of the trade. With one hand, he whipped the cable, snapping the end around the leader's arm.

The huge Nomanchulator reared and shrieked. All at once, the swarm attacked, overwhelming White Blade. The cable slid through his hand, and the leader freed itself. I thought White Blade might be finished then, but his sword flashed faster than seemed possible, fending off the swarm.

"There's not much time," Kiana pressed. "Come on, J.T. Prove that you're the one."

"And then this will be over? I can do anything?"

She stared at me with a fierce, almost hungry look. "Then you'll become what you've always dreamed of being."

I drew my sword and jumped into the alley before I lost my nerve.

The swarm surrounded me as soon as I landed. I cut down three of the Nomanchulators closest to White Blade. He shot me a wary glance. Instead of fighting him, I helped him fend off the swarm. White Blade nodded, seeming to accept our alliance. We fought side by side, pushing back the Nomanchulators.

White Blade went after the leader again. He whipped his cable around the creature's neck, and the huge Nomanchulator thrashed. I grabbed the cable and threw my weight against it to help him, but still we couldn't hold the creature. The Nomanchulator fixed its dead black eyes on me, and a numbing chill filled my body. Even together, I wasn't sure that we could defeat them. The swarm was simply too large.

"Over there!" White Blade called, his voice muffled by the scarf that covered his face. He gestured to a nearby fire hydrant, and I guessed his plan. If we could wrap the end of the cable around the hydrant, the leader would be stuck while we picked off the rest.

White Blade dropped his sword and grabbed the cable with both hands. He braced his feet against the curb. Together we pulled, freeing enough slack for me to wrap around the hydrant.

"Hurry!" he gasped.

I tied a slipknot in the slack. Then I looped the cable around White Blade's neck and let go.

Through the gap in the scarf that covered his face, I saw his eyes go wide. A look of shock? Betrayal? Pain?

He clawed at the cable, tugging his scarf down. Recognition stabbed my chest. His eyes, nose, mouth, and other features were the same as mine, sure as staring in a mirror.

Then he was gone—dragged by his neck into the swarm.

Nomanchulators engulfed his body, eager to feed. In the center stood the leader, its long mosquito mouth poised over White Blade's face. My face.

"Well done!" shouted Kiana from the roof of a building overlooking the alley. "I knew you'd help us." Her voice fractured into a cold, insectual laugh, and her eyes became the same dead black as the Nomanchulators.'

I woke, horrified and sickened by what I'd done.

CRaSh

JESS ARRIVED TUESDAY EVENING. She stood on the front steps in a black skirt and dress shoes, even though snow blanketed the ground. Her shirt was buttoned high enough to cover the Japanese characters tattooed on her chest. She kept her dark hair in a ponytail, with a few loose strands arranged over her cheek and eyebrow piercing. To top it off, she held a bouquet of irises between both hands like a flower girl in a wedding.

"Here you go, Mrs. Turner," she said, handing Moms the bouquet.

My jaw dropped. I'd never heard Jess call anyone Mrs.—not even teachers, who she usually had perverted nicknames for.

"Goodness, flowers in winter," Moms said. "You are the sweetest thing." She hustled Jess into the kitchen to get a drink of hot chocolate and warm up. Jess smiled at me as she passed, but with Moms talking up a storm, we didn't have a moment to ourselves.

"Now, you have to tell me, *Jessica*," Moms said, "how do you get your hair to do that? It's adorable. Do you think I could get away with it?" Moms pulled her hair back into a ponytail, letting a few strands fall onto her cheek. Her hair was longer and curlier than Jess's, so it looked frumpy. "Or am I too old?"

"Too old? I can't believe you'd say that, Mrs. Turner," Jess replied. "You look great."

"Please, call me Hannah. If you call me Mrs. Turner, I'll have to check into a nursing home."

The two of them went back and forth like that, talking about haircuts and fondling each other's clothes. Moms offered to give Jess the "grand tour" (which only lasted a few minutes since our house isn't very big). She explained the "themes" she had for decorating each room, and how she planned on getting the couch re-covered and finding new curtains. I waited for Jess to roll her eyes and yawn. Instead, she kept encouraging Moms, acting interested at all the right moments.

"You have such beautiful things," Jess said.

"It's a work in progress," Moms replied. "I keep getting ideas from magazines."

Dad worked in the basement until dinner was ready. "I won't shake your hand," he said when he finally emerged. He held up his hands to show Jess the grease stains he'd gotten from repairing a TV. That was his hobby—he had a whole wall of old TVs in the basement that he'd fixed. I don't know why he bothered. No one ever watched them.

We ate in the dining room. Moms had made me set the table with her "silver" and "nice" plates before Jess arrived. Jess commented on how pretty things looked, even though the dishes had been out of style for at least ten years. I figured Jess's comment must be ironic, but Moms didn't catch it. She lapped the praise right up and went on to describe her plans for redecorating the dining room, and what light fixtures she wanted, and how muted colors were in, rambling on and on as if changing the color of the walls would magically turn our drab house into a palace.

"Who cares about crown moldings?" I said.

Moms glared at me.

"Actually, I like hearing about design," Jess said. "I'm thinking of majoring in design."

"See, honey?" Moms replied. "I know what I'm saying."

Dad muttered something about how all the changes would cost a lot. Which got Moms talking about her business selling Avon.

"Oh, I love Avon," Jess cooed.

"Me, too. It won't be long before I'm driving a pink Caddy."

"That's Mary Kay," I said.

"Avon gives out pink Cadillacs, too. Or is it a red one? Red's better."

"Red's my favorite color," Jess said. "But it has to be the right shade of red. I can't stand weak reds."

Moms started listing all the different shades of red that Avon carried. I kept looking at Jess, trying to share some inside joke with her, only she didn't look back. Luckily, there wasn't any dessert, so we were able to slip away on the pretense of getting ice cream.

Moms raised her eyebrows. "Ice cream? In winter?"

"Let them go," Dad said.

I couldn't leave the house fast enough. Jess had borrowed her dad's car—a green Ford with splotches of rust around the wheel wells. She offered to let me drive since I knew the town. "It's no race car," she said, handing me the keys.

"I'll be gentle." I hopped behind the wheel, neglecting to mention that legally I wasn't supposed to drive after dark with a learner's permit. We went to 7-Eleven and bought a pint of Chunky Monkey, then sat in the parking lot, eating it with plastic spoons.

"Told you I was good with parents," Jess said.

"Great. I hope you win a flipping Oscar."

"I think your mom likes me."

"Sorry about that," I said, prying out a fudge nugget.

"About what?"

"My mom."

"Why? She's nice. Your parents aren't what I expected at all."

I nearly choked on the ice cream. "How so?"

Jess shrugged. "After some of the stories you told me, I pictured your dad passed out on the couch with a case of Bud Light on his belly while your mom chain-smoked and ran a phone sex line."

"I wish."

"You're lucky to have nice parents," Jess said.

"Nice is the same as boring."

"Believe me, I'd take boring over messed-up and missing any day."

I stared out the window. Jess had told me once that she hadn't seen her mother in years. Compared to what she'd been through, my problems seemed childish.

"You okay?" she asked.

"Yeah."

Jess put her hand on my thigh. "So what do you do around here for fun?"

I thought of my dreams, and how I'd betrayed White Blade. My leg jerked, shaking her hand off.

She gave me a perplexed look.

"Let's go someplace," I said.

"We are someplace."

"You want to go someplace that isn't a parking lot?"

"Fine." She shoved the lid back on the ice cream and tossed the pint onto the floor. "It's your call."

I drove for a while on backstreets. There weren't many

cars out, and the sky had this eerie, orangish glow from the streetlights reflecting off the clouds. I headed out of town, pretending that I was leaving for good.

"Where are we going?" Jess asked.

"This place I know."

"Where?"

"It's just a few miles," I said, even though I had no clue where I was heading. The road I'd turned onto didn't have any signs, and there was nothing but cornfields on both sides. Fog swirled in the headlights, making it hard to see more than thirty feet ahead. "Just wait," I added, trying to sound mysterious. "You'll love it."

"Do you even know where you're going?"

"Of course." I gripped the wheel, hoping that something would come up—some park or abandoned barn. Some place worth seeing. If I could just keep driving, things had to change and I could tear away from my past and shed my nightmares like they were all part of a lame costume I'd been wearing. Then I'd be reborn as someone different. Someone better.

Jess slumped in her seat, putting her feet on the dash. "You're so full of it," she said.

"Trust me, okay? It's going to be great."

"What is?"

"Don't you want to get away from all this?"

"Get away from what?" she asked.

"From everything."

"From me?"

I thought of my nightmares again. The deadening buzz of the Nomanchulators filled my head, pushing closer now. "You don't understand," I said. "People are after me."

"You're such a liar."

"I'm not lying." I pressed on the gas, and the road blurred beneath us. The stubble of cut-down cornfields on both sides sprawled into an endless gray emptiness. There had to be something more than this.

A yellow sign with a curving black arrow emerged out of the fog.

"Slow down!" Jess yelled.

I turned the wheel, but it was too late—the car kept sliding forward. We slammed into the ditch and spun across the frozen mud. Snowflakes sparkled in the headlights with sudden, exquisite clarity. I don't know if I had my foot on the brake or the gas, but it seemed to take a long time before we finally stopped.

Each heartbeat shook my chest, rattling me awake. Jess stayed silent, staring straight ahead.

"Wow," I said, when my breathing had calmed enough to talk.

Jess didn't respond.

I reached for her hand, but she pulled it away. "Are you all right?" I asked.

She buried her face in her arms and cried.

Part IV

*. . . this thing of darkness I
Acknowledge mine.*

—*THE TEMPEST,* ACT 5, SCENE 1

Welcome Back

WE ENDED UP HAVING TO CALL a tow truck to pull her dad's car out, but Jess had roadside assistance, so it wasn't a big deal. Luckily the car seemed to drive okay, although it had gotten pretty muddy. Jess wouldn't speak to me for the whole two hours it took to get the car out and drop me off. I e-mailed her a few times in the days that followed, offering to pay for anything wrong with the car. She didn't reply. Ghost44 didn't log on again either, so the second half of my break ended up being lonelier than the first.

Even my dreams were lonely. I didn't want to see the guides anymore—not after how they'd tricked me into binding White Blade. Unfortunately, I couldn't stop dreaming. Nearly every night, I wandered the empty streets of the city alone, terrified that it was only a matter of time before the Nomanchulators caught me.

The one good thing that happened was that I did okay on my exams. No one from the administration called after my grades were reported, so I figured I wasn't kicked out. I couldn't wait to return to ASMA.

Dad drove me back to campus early Sunday afternoon. He offered to help me carry my stuff into the dorm, but I only had a backpack full of books and a laundry basket of clothes that Moms had washed and folded for me.

"I got it," I told Dad, slinging my backpack over my shoulder and grabbing the basket.

Dad pulled a plastic grocery bag out of the trunk. "Your mom packed some snacks for you."

Through the plastic, I could see the outline of several ramen packets. "Can you put them in the basket?"

Dad looked at the door. "You sure you can carry all this?"

"No problem," I said.

He must have sensed that I wanted to be on my own, because he didn't argue with me. Instead, he tucked the bag into the corner of the laundry basket and gave my shoulder a pat. "Stay out of trouble," he said.

I told him good-bye and hurried into my dorm, eager to see friends, and hang out, and be someone again, but when I entered my room, things looked different.

It took me a moment to realize that my bed was missing. Everything—the mattress, sheets, pillow, comforter—had disappeared. Dickie's bed was gone, too, and I couldn't find any of the clothes I'd left in my closet. I was about to check the number on the door to make sure I had the right room, but duh—my posters still covered the walls.

Maybe I'd been kicked out after all, I thought. The RCs might have put my stuff in boxes, and Dickie might have moved to a different room. Everyone probably knew I wasn't supposed to be here anymore.

I searched my room again. Then I opened the bathroom door. All the missing things, including my mattress, had been jammed into the shower.

I had to admit the prank was pretty impressive, but my relief at realizing that I hadn't been expelled quickly changed to cursing when I opened the glass door and water poured out. The Steves had turned the shower on.

I surveyed the mess. If I left it for later, I wouldn't have anything to sleep on, so I pulled off all the wet bedding and headed for the laundry room.

Sunny was standing outside my door when I returned. "I don't think he's back yet," I said, figuring that she was there to see Dickie.

"Okay if I hang out with you while I wait?"

"Sure. If you don't mind the flood."

She raised her eyebrows. I propped open the door and showed her the pile of mattresses and clothes in the shower.

"So *that's* how you do laundry."

"Very funny." I wrung out a pair of boxers. "I think the Steves did it."

"Look, James, if you've got a bed-wetting problem, that's okay. You don't have to blame it on someone else." She giggled and patted my back.

I didn't mind the teasing from Sunny. She never got mean about it, and she had a beautiful laugh. Being around her brightened my mood.

I draped my boxers over the shower rod to dry. Then I got some hangers out of my closet for the other clothes. The mattresses I propped against our bed frames to air out. Sunny gave me a hand, hanging my jeans and shirts.

"You don't have to help," I said.

She kept hanging things. "I don't mind. Anyway, I feel a little guilty about all this."

"Why?"

"I think I might have started this whole prank war thingy."

"How?"

"I dated Steve Lacone at the beginning of the year."

"You're kidding?"

"Nope," she said. "We only went out for a few days. Then I started hanging with you guys, which pissed Steve off."

"Hold on. Is that why they pelted us with water balloons?"

"Probably." Sunny draped a few wet socks over the shower bar.

I thought of the water balloon and shaving cream fight we'd had at the beginning of the year, right after I'd dyed my hair with Sunny. Anything had seemed possible then. "Okay," I said, accepting that Sunny and Steve had dated. "So why'd you split up?"

"Don't tell anyone this, but no matter what we did or where we went, Steve Dennon came with us."

"That's not a surprise. Steve Dennon worships Steve Lacone."

"Yeah. But the weird thing is, one night Steve and I were by the pond, messing around . . ."

"Steve Lacone, right?"

Sunny slapped my shoulder. "Of course!"

"Just checking."

"So we were making out," she continued, "and Steve groaned, *Oh, Steve!*"

"Whoa!"

"No kidding. I didn't know if he was saying, *Oh, Steve!* meaning himself, like he thought he was so great. Or if he was saying, *Oh, Steve!* like he was fantasizing about kissing Steve Dennon."

"So what'd you do?"

"Nothing. But that was the last time I walked the pond with him. When a guy calls out someone else's name in the heat of passion, even if it's his own name, it's not a good sign."

I tried to imagine a situation where, in the heat of passion, I might gasp, *Oh, James!*

"What about you?" Sunny asked. "What happened between you and Jess?"

"I think we broke up."

"Uh . . . yeah. She said you turned into a suicidal maniac and crashed her dad's car."

"She told you that?"

"I heard her and Rachel talking in our commons earlier. She seemed kind of pissed."

"Did she say anything else?" I asked, hoping that Jess hadn't told anyone about my parents, or what a phony I was.

Sunny shook her head. "Not that I heard. You want to tell me about it?"

I wrung out a shirt and draped it over a hanger. In a way, it was a relief not to have to worry about impressing Jess anymore. "Guess I wanted to break up with her," I said.

"So you crashed her car?"

"Uh-huh."

Sunny stopped hanging clothes and leaned against the door frame. "If I dared you to do something, would you do it?"

"Maybe."

"It's not a bad thing," she said. "But you have to promise me you'll do it before I tell you what it is."

"Why?"

"Promise me first."

"Okay," I said. "What do you dare me to do?"

"Go see Chuck."

I drew back, confused. "The shrink?"

Sunny nodded. "I'm worried about you."

"Don't be."

"I'm not the only one who's worried. Dickie is, too."

I scowled, annoyed that they'd been talking about me. "I'm the sanest person I know."

Sunny put her hand on my arm. "You just crashed your girlfriend's car to break up with her."

"That was an accident."

"What about these?" She turned my arm, exposing the cuts on the other side. "Are these accidents?"

I pulled away. "They're nothing."

"If they're nothing, then why are you afraid to talk to Chuck?"

"I'm not afraid."

"Please," Sunny urged. "I'll go with you."

"Fine," I said. "If it means that much to you, I'll go. Once."

She gave me a huge, Sunny smile. "Thanks!" she said, and kissed my cheek.

TRappeD

THE FAINT SCENT OF COFFEE drifted on the air. At first, that didn't seem significant until I realized where I was—stuck in the dream again. I followed the scent to the diner where I'd first met the guides.

The place looked abandoned. All the windows had been broken, and the lights were out. Cobwebs tickled my face and glass shards crunched beneath my feet as I walked through the door. No waitress greeted me. I was about to leave when I saw something move.

It was a man with bushy white hair hunched at the counter. He turned over a mug beside him and filled it with steaming coffee from a thermos. "Might as well sit," he said. "Drink it while it's hot."

I cupped the mug in my hands. Coffee grounds swirled around the top, but the smell was irresistible. "Got any sugar?" I asked.

"Nope," the man said. "It's coffee. It's supposed to taste bitter."

I took a sip, cringing.

"Thought you might come back here," the man said. His face was tan, and wrinkles radiated around the corners of his eyes. I vaguely remembered him from my waking life.

"Liam?" I asked.

The man shrugged.

"You're Liam," I said. "Sage's father. I met you at that picnic."

"Call me what you like. It's your show." He sipped his coffee and nodded to himself. "You sure have made a mess of things, haven't you?"

"I didn't do this," I said, glancing around the diner.

"That's right. You're not responsible for anything that's happened, are you?" Liam turned to face me. "I saw you come here the first time, you know. You could have sat with anyone in the room. You had a choice then." He rubbed the white stubble on his cheek. "Bet you didn't even notice me."

I shook my head.

"I was sitting right here when you came in." He

tapped the counter. "I'd even kept that stool empty for you."

I thought back to the last time I'd been in the diner. Several figures had been at the counter, but I hadn't given them much consideration.

"Yup. You chose them," Liam continued. "You walked over to their booth and plopped down with them of your own free will. Why? Because she was pretty? Because he looked cool? Because you wanted to be like them?"

"I don't know. They called me over."

"Baloney." Liam took a sip of his coffee and clanked the empty cup onto the saucer. "They didn't call you over. You weren't tricked into helping the Nomanchulators. You chose to do it."

"I didn't know who they were."

"You didn't want to know," he said.

I lifted my coffee, then thought better of it and set the cup back down. The little I'd drunk burned like battery acid in my belly. "I'm so tired of this," I muttered. "I hate being stuck here."

"Then why don't you leave?"

"I can't leave. This city doesn't end."

"If you say so."

"Hold on. Do you know a way out?"

"Naw. I've been here my whole life. But . . ."

"But what?"

"You haven't." He squinted at me. "Wherever you go, there you are, right, James?"

"So there's a way out?"

"You're barking up the wrong tree." He unscrewed the thermos and refilled his cup. "The question you should be asking is how you got yourself into this mess. Figure that out, and you might be able to leave."

I pushed away from the counter and stood.

"Good luck finding a way out of your own head," Liam muttered. "'Cause that's the pickle, isn't it?"

Secret to Success

IN PHYSICS, DR. CHOI ASSIGNED US new lab groups for the spring semester. It was just my luck that I got put with Cheese, Muppet, and the Ice Queen.

We were supposed to pull our desks together and work on a problem set with our new groups. Cheese slumped in his seat as if it pained him to move, while Muppet scuttled about trying to get our desks to form a perfect square. Ellie seemed tired. There were faint shadows under her eyes that gave her a bruised look, but that didn't stop her from being completely gorgeous. And stuck-up. As soon as I came over, she set her back to me, her perfect posture impenetrable as a wall.

Great, I thought. *One more girl who hates me.*

I didn't know why *she* was pissed. If anyone should have been angry, it was me. After all, the last time I'd seen her, she was walking away, leaving me to freeze by the pond. At the very least, I thought she'd apologize for calling security and getting me suspended, instead of acting like my mere existence offended her.

Ellie asked Muppet how his break had been.

The poor kid got so nervous talking to her that he rambled on and on about the "blaring inconsistencies" in some alien invasion movie he'd seen. "And then," he sputtered, "when the spaceships went by, there was this whooshing sound. Like there could be sound in space, when everyone knows waves don't travel through a vacuum." He laughed, as if he'd made a very funny joke.

"Exactly," I said. "I was totally buying the fact that aliens were popping out of people's bellies until the sound of the spaceships ruined it all."

Ellie ignored my sarcasm. "You're right. I hate it when movies do that," she said to Muppet. Then she smiled at Cheese. "What about you, Cheese?" she asked, completely dissing me. "How was your break?"

I talked with Cheese about it on the way back to our dorm. "Ice Queen didn't even say hello to me," I said. "I mean, how stuck-up can you get?"

Cheese shrugged.

"I'm serious. Tell me you saw what I'm talking about. She totally hates me."

"She's just shy, man," Cheese said. "That's her thing."

"She's not shy about talking with you. Or Muppet."

"We were in her chemistry group last semester. She knows us. Anyhow, what's the big deal? Are you into her?"

"The Ice Queen?" I smirked. "No way. I just want our physics group to go well."

"Of course. Physics." Cheese swiped his ID across the dorm sensor so we could enter. "Like the study of parabolic curves. Or the heat produced from the friction between two bodies. I'm all about physics."

"The fact that you're trying to eroticize parabolic equations—that's messed up."

"Physics, biology, chemistry," Cheese said, "it's all sex."

"You're sick."

"That's my secret to success—relate everything to sex and suddenly it's interesting. How else do you stay awake when Ms. Krup drones on about covalent bonds?" He unlocked the door to his room and yawned. The shades were drawn, and the stuffy air smelled vaguely of rotting food and sweaty sneakers. "I'm gonna take a nap," Cheese said, pushing a pile of dirty clothes off his mattress.

"Dude, you're always sleeping."

"It's my hobby."

Cheese dropped his backpack onto a pizza box and flopped into bed. I lingered by the door. "Do you remember your dreams?" I asked.

"Sometimes," he said.

"What are they like?"

"Strange . . . good . . . dirty . . . They're dreams, man."

"You ever get stuck in them?"

He leaned on his elbow and looked at me. "How so?"

"I don't know." I paused, not sure how to explain it. Cheese kept looking at me, waiting for me to say more. "It's like I'm living this other life in my head, and I can't get out of it," I said. "Sometimes I think my dreams are taking over. Does that sound crazy?"

"Naw," Cheese replied. "Everyone's stuck in their heads."

"They are?"

"Definitely. Only not everyone's aware of it."

"How do you know?"

"You can't know," Cheese said. "That's the whole point. It's impossible to know what's going on in someone else's head, because everything we know is in our own head."

I pictured a bunch of goldfish in bags, floating around in one big tank, their self-contained worlds bumping into each other's. It reminded me of what ghost44 had said— that no one ever really knows anyone else. "Doesn't that bother you?" I asked.

"No way, man." Cheese grinned. "Would you want to see the sick stuff that goes on in my head?"

"I'll pass."

"I mean, where do you think you go when you die, right?"

"Huh?"

"When you die," he repeated, as though the connection between dreams and death should be totally obvious.

I stood there, dumbfounded.

"Take this lamp," Cheese said, turning on the reading light next to his bed. "Say the light is consciousness, okay?" He flicked the light off and on. "You can turn the light off, but the lamp's only aware when it's on, so it thinks it's on all the time. You get it?"

"I guess."

"In order to *know* that you're dead, you have to be conscious," he explained. "But if you're conscious, then you're not dead. The only thing you can know is being alive, so that's eternity." He flicked the light off and on again. "Think about it. We might be dead right now, but we don't know it. We keep dreaming ourselves alive."

"So I'm dreaming you up right now, talking to me?" I asked.

"Maybe. Maybe I'm not talking at all," Cheese said. "Maybe you only think I am, but you don't hear *me*. Not really. Your whole experience of hearing me is just neurons flashing in your brain. It's all in your head. It's all dreams, man. Day. Night. Eternity. Dreams within dreams. Life is but a dream."

"So we're stuck in our heads forever?"

Cheese shrugged.

I imagined being trapped in my dreams with the Nomanchulators for eternity. "That's depressing."

"It doesn't have to be," he said. "You could believe in nice things, like heaven. And I'm not talking about the boring, religious one with the harps and angels and crap, but some cushy afterlife with lots of ladies, because if you believe in it, then you make space for it to happen. Get it?"

"Kind of," I said, although I still didn't like the idea of always being stuck in my head. "It seems lonely. What if, when we die, part of us lives on and that's how we know that we're dead?"

"If part of you lives on, then you're not really dead," Cheese countered.

"Well, what if the part that lives on is us but not us. Like maybe we're part of something bigger than ourselves."

"Could be."

"Then we're not stuck in our heads forever?"

"If that's what you want to believe. Yeah."

My brow knitted.

"You imprison yourself, or you free yourself," Cheese said. "It's all a matter of perspective."

"So what do you believe?" I asked. "Are we all imprisoned in our own little worlds or are we all connected somehow?"

Cheese turned off the lamp and plopped onto his pillow. "Both," he said, closing his eyes. "I believe in sleep. And sex."

I kept standing there, but he didn't say anything more. After a minute, I turned and started to leave.

"She's funny, you know," he said. "Got a nice sense of humor. You wouldn't think that, but she does."

"Who?"

"The . . . Ice . . . Queen . . ." Cheese mumbled in a slurred, sleepy voice. "Chemistry," he groaned, like he was describing some perverted fantasy. "Covalent bondage . . . electron pair theory . . . carbon-on-carbon bonds . . . exothermic reactions . . . oh, yeah."

Ghost

johnnyrotten: You there?

ghost44: Maybe.

johnnyrotten: A response! I tried messaging you like twenty times before, but I got nada.

ghost44: I've been taking a break lately.

johnnyrotten: From what?

ghost44: Haunting people.

johnnyrotten: Uh-oh. Too much snickerdoodle and spinach over break?

ghost44: Yes, actually. But that's not why.

johnnyrotten: Then why?

ghost44: I think I'm losing my ghostly edge.

johnnyrotten: How so?

ghost44: For starters, I keep trying to stop a friend from hurting himself, but he keeps doing incredibly stupid stuff like jumping into frozen ponds and crashing cars.

johnnyrotten: You heard about that?

ghost44: Only the whole school's heard about that, Speed Racer. Do you miss Jess?

johnnyrotten: Hmmm . . . a little. I miss being with someone, but I think you were right. We weren't very good for each other.

ghost44: I'm always right. It's the curse of being a ghost—to be right yet have no one listen.

johnnyrotten: I listen to you.

ghost44: No, you don't. If you did, you'd stop making the same mistakes over and over again.

johnnyrotten: At least I make mistakes. You won't even try to be with the person you like.

ghost44: That's because I can't be with him.

johnnyrotten: I don't buy it. Maybe things won't turn out exactly the way you want them to, but some things might surprise you. They might even be better than you thought. The only way to know is to take a risk.

ghost44: Like speeding on an icy road?

johnnyrotten: I mean a good risk. Like going up to the person and being honest with them.

ghost44: If only it were that easy.

johnnyrotten: Why isn't it? You keep talking about breaking through all the superficial crap that keeps people apart, but the truth is, you keep yourself apart. You're just like Emily Dickinson, hiding behind her door.

ghost44: That's not true.

johnnyrotten: Then why won't you try to be with the person you like?

ghost44: I already told you—it won't work out.

johnnyrotten: Why?

ghost44: Because there's this gap between who I am and who people see. I can't be myself in person.

johnnyrotten: Can't or won't? It's your choice—you imprison yourself or you free yourself.

ghost44: It's not that simple.

johnnyrotten: But what if it is? What if all it takes to cross the gap is to reach out and have someone reach back?

ghost44: And if the person doesn't reach back?

johnnyrotten: Then they don't reach back. Only you have to believe that they will, or you're not really reaching.

ghost44: I can't believe you're giving me relationship advice.

johnnyrotten: I'm just saying, maybe it's better to try and mess up than not to try at all.

ghost44: I have tried.

johnnyrotten: So try again.

ghost44: And if it doesn't work? If I lose hope and fall into the gap?

johnnyrotten: Then you have to look for someone with freakishly long arms who can pull you out—like the world's tallest man who saved those dolphins.

ghost44: ?

johnnyrotten: It's true. These dolphins swallowed some plastic trash, so the veterinarians called in this incredibly tall Mongolian goat herder to reach in and pull it out.

ghost44: You were doing well before you brought up the dolphins.

johnnyrotten: Sorry. But you get what I'm saying, right? You have to try.

ghost44: Fine. I'll try again to reach across the gap.

johnnyrotten: And will you tell me what happens?

ghost44: That depends.

johnnyrotten: On what?

ghost44: On whether there's a part of me left that still trusts people.

johnnyrotten: Good luck, ghost.

ghost44: Good night, James.

Chuck

SUNNY KEPT BUGGING ME about my promise to see Chuck. I put it off a few times, but I knew that the more I avoided it, the bigger deal it would become. On Tuesday, I finally agreed to go with her during lunch, when most students were in the cafeteria. Even though I'd been to Health and Student Services before to get a Band-Aid or an aspirin, this time felt different. I worried that someone might see me going in there and think, "Yup, he's a nut job."

Saxophone music murmured from the radio on Linda's bookshelf—the sort of bland "soft jazz" that businesses piped into offices to make us calm, productive robots. I stood, my skin crawling from the music, while Linda finished typing something into her computer.

"Hi, Sunny," she said. "And James—been a while since you've dropped by."

I took a dark chocolate Hershey's Kiss from the candy jar on Linda's desk. "If I'd known these were here, I would have come more often," I said. "Dark chocolate's my favorite."

"I'll keep that in mind." Linda tapped a few more keys on her computer, then leaned back. "What can I help you two with?"

Sunny explained that I was there to schedule an appointment with Chuck. Linda nodded, suddenly very professional. She gave me a form on a clipboard to fill out.

I looked over the form while Sunny read a magazine. The questions ranged from the normal name and date of birth to things that I knew better than to answer honestly, like: "How often do you drink alcoholic beverages?" and "Check off which substances you have used: Hallucinogens, Marijuana, Amphetamines, Cocaine, Depressants, Other." I checked off "Other" and wrote in "Tater Tot casserole."

On the back, the form listed different behaviors and asked me to "check all that apply." The list had a bunch of hard-core crazy things on it like "hyperventilate in open spaces," "suicidal thoughts," "pulling hair out," "feeling guilty when I eat," "purging," and so on. I looked through it twice. "Lonely" wasn't an option. Neither was "bad dreams." They must have been too common to count. I thought about not checking anything, then, on a whim, I checked the box marked "cutting."

I gave Linda the form. She scanned the front and back. "So," she said, giving me a long look, "how many classes have you missed?"

"What?"

"The cutting," Linda said. "It says here you're cutting classes."

"Oh," I said. "Too many."

Chuck didn't have time to see me that day, so I had to come back for an appointment on Thursday. I considered skipping it after Linda's brilliant assessment, but Sunny might have found out.

When I arrived on Thursday, Linda sent me straight in. Chuck's office resembled a run-down living room with an old brown couch and two orange chairs arranged around a beat-up coffee table. Books covered one wall, and the others were decorated with cheap art prints. A row of filing cabinets stood in the corner with a spindly plant on top—all yellow leaves and bare branches.

Chuck sat in one of the padded orange chairs. He had his feet on the coffee table and a stack of papers in his lap. This was one of his bold, eyeless days. His lid hung limp over the empty socket. I had a ridiculous image of him lifting the lid, and instead of an empty hole, there'd be a mystical jewel that he'd use to hypnotize me. Any second now, he might lift the lid and stare at me with his witching eye and I'd be gaga.

"Take off your coat," Chuck said, glancing at me with his good eye. "Make yourself comfortable."

I did, since it was pretty hot in his office. Chuck made no indication about whether I should sit in the chair or on the couch. I figured it might be a test, so I sat in the chair and stared straight at him. No way was I going to lie down on the couch and talk about my mother.

Chuck stared back. The eyelid over his missing eye didn't move at all. "A lefty, huh?" he said. "Southpaw."

"Yeah," I replied, wondering if my handwriting on the form could have given me away. People didn't usually notice I was left-handed until they saw me write or throw. "How can you tell?"

"Most of the scars are on your right arm."

I wanted to kick myself for taking off my coat. "It's from martial arts," I said, crossing my arms. "I spar a lot, and sometimes we use swords."

Chuck nodded, like he believed me. "Do you enjoy fighting?"

"Not really."

"Then why do you do it?"

"I don't." I fidgeted in the chair, trying to find a comfortable position on the sunken cushion. "I was kidding about the fights."

Chuck nodded again. "Sorry. I tend to take everything people say seriously. Otherwise, what's the point of talking?"

He paused, as if expecting an answer. I knew this trick—stay silent and let the other person mess up. I looked around the room, scanning the titles on the bookshelves.

"So you're not a fighter?" He arched his eyebrows, as if he knew I wasn't being straight with him.

I thought about the stories I'd told people at the beginning of the year. Maybe Chuck had heard some of the rumors about me. I opened my mouth to explain, but what could I say? That I'd lied to everyone to make myself seem interesting? That I'd completely reinvented myself and now I wasn't sure what was true and what I'd made up? The lines had blurred. It was too late now to go back.

"I try not to fight anymore," I said.

"Then how'd you get the cuts?"

"Maybe I want to kill myself."

Chuck didn't flinch. "Is that what you'd like me to believe?"

"No."

"Good. It's not funny."

"I wasn't trying to be funny."

"Fair enough," Chuck said. "You're testing me, which is fine, but I should level with you. I don't think you're suicidal. You're smart enough to know that if you really wanted to kill yourself, the cuts would go the other way—lengthwise along your vein."

I looked at the thin white scars that crossed the inside of my forearm. "Linda thought I was cutting classes."

Chuck shrugged. "People don't like to acknowledge things that disturb them."

"And you're different?"

"Listen, James," he said, putting his feet on the floor and leaning toward me. "I believe there's nothing too terrible to talk about. But there are many things too terrible *not* to talk about. What we don't talk about, what we don't face, often comes back to haunt us. So why are you here?"

He did it again—stared at me with his one eye and arched his eyebrow, like he knew I was hiding something.

"I'll be honest with you," I said. "I only came because a friend dared me to see you."

"I see. And you couldn't turn down a dare?"

"Guess not."

"What do you make of that?"

I smirked, refusing to fall for such an obvious ploy. Instead of answering, I looked at the pictures on the walls.

The guidance counselor's office at my old high school had been covered with inspirational posters of mountain scenes or ocean waves with things like PERSEVERANCE and CHARACTER defined on them. Chuck's posters were only a little better than those. A van Gogh of a field with crows, a café scene, a Picasso of the man with the blue guitar— your cliché "classy" art posters.

"Nice pictures," I said.

"Thanks."

I stared at the van Gogh. The yellow wheat under the dark blue sky glowed bright as sunshine. An art teacher

I'd had a few years ago had told me the crows in the picture symbolized madness. "You know van Gogh was crazy when he painted that," I said. "He used to stick the dirty brushes in his mouth to wet them, and the yellow paint had lead in it. So all those pretty colors poisoned him."

"Is that so?" Chuck seemed genuinely interested, as if he'd never heard that before. I could tell things were going nowhere.

"Hey," I said, preparing to stand, "I appreciate you being here, but I don't want to waste your time."

Chuck glanced at his watch. "Your appointment doesn't end until one."

"I don't have anything to talk about. Honest. There are people with real problems who need to be in here."

"And your problems aren't *real*?"

The way he said it made me cringe. "Look, I can deal with my problems," I said, "so there's no point in me wasting your time."

Chuck wrinkled his forehead, which made the eyelid over the missing eye lift the slightest bit. "It's my time. Right now, I'd like to talk with you. In fact, you're exactly the sort of person I'm here to help."

"I don't need help."

"That's a stupid thing to say."

I glared at him. "You think I'm stupid?"

"Not at all. I've no doubt that you're smart enough to fool me. And yourself." He leaned forward with his hands on his knees. Even sitting down, he looked big. "For instance, you might fool yourself into believing that you don't need help."

"I don't need help. That's what I'm saying. I only came because of a dare."

"Okay. But can your life be better?"

"Sure," I said. "Everyone's life can be better."

"Not everyone cuts themselves." He folded his thick hands in his lap, exposing the blurry blue line of a tattoo on his forearm. I couldn't make out what it was. Probably an anchor, given his clichéd taste. "That worries me, James. Why do you hurt yourself?"

Great. Just what I needed—a two-hundred-pound-middle-aged-one-eyed-tattooed shrink worried about me. "If you think I'm trying to hurt myself, you've got it all wrong."

"Then enlighten me."

"Number one, I don't cut myself to hurt myself. I mean, it hurts, but I'm not afraid of pain. I can control it. And number two, I like myself. I really do. The only reason I cut myself is to feel something."

He folded his hands beneath his chin. "So you're beyond being hurt?"

"I can deal with it."

"Is that right?"

"Look, I'm not afraid of pain. I'm in control."

"Control?"

"Of myself. Everything's great."

"Then why do you have to cut yourself to feel?"

I glanced away, not wanting Chuck to see that he'd stumped me. "Your plant's dying," I said.

"So it is."

He didn't say anything else, and neither did I. The buzz of the Nomanchulators hovered at the edge of my awareness.

"Can I go now?"

"Sure." Chuck raised his hands in a no-one's-stopping-you gesture. "It's your decision. If you don't want to be here, I can't make you stay."

I headed for the door.

"Hey, James," he called before I made it out. "I'm just curious. What are you running from?"

"I'm not running from anything."

"I think you are." He fixed his eye on me.

A chill crept up my spine as the buzz of the Nomanchulators grew louder. Lately, their deadening sound had begun to spill out into my waking life, numbing me.

"We can talk about it next week." Chuck reached for his planner, eager to put me down in a box. "I'll pencil you in for the same time."

"Don't bother," I said. "Thanks anyway."

Linda's radio was turned down so low when I left that I could barely hear the music beneath the buzzing swarm. She flipped through a stack of papers. By her overly industrious movements, I could tell she'd been listening in.

"Need a pass?" she asked.

I shook my head, anxious to get out of there.

Someone else was in the room, waiting for Chuck. She kept her face buried in a magazine, trying to remain anonymous.

"You can go in now," Linda said to the girl. "Chuck's waiting."

The Ice Queen set her magazine down, brushed her skirt flat, and stood. I remembered how I'd run into her here previously. All at once the full significance of her presence sank in. She hadn't been getting a Band-Aid, as she'd claimed. She was seeing Chuck. Ms. Perfect had problems.

Our eyes met. For a moment her usual icy confidence was gone. It was like peeking behind a movie set and discovering that the walls that looked so solid to the audience were only painted sheets of cardboard, held up by a few flimsy struts.

I opened my mouth to tell her something, but I didn't know what.

Ellie slipped past me and ducked into Chuck's office. It wasn't until a few weeks later that I realized what I should have said. But by then, of course, it was too late.

STUPID

THAT NIGHT, I COULDN'T SLEEP. The Nomanchulators still seemed close and I didn't want to risk dreaming of the city again. After thrashing in bed for over an hour, I finally got up to find something to eat. The only snacks I had left were a dozen packets of ramen. I considered fixing a bowl, but the thought of eating more fake-chicken-flavored noodles made me want to hurl. Then, in a stroke of late-night-snack-attack brilliance, an idea came to me—the prank to end all pranks.

"Hey, Dickie," I said, shaking him. "Wake up, man."

He grunted and tried to bat my hand away.

"Dude, wake up! It's important."

Dickie struggled onto his elbow, blinking against the light I'd turned on. "What's wrong?"

"Nothing's wrong," I said. "I've got an idea."

He frowned. "I was sleeping."

"Come on—it's the best prank ever."

"I have a test tomorrow."

"So?"

"So I need to sleep," he said, annoyed. "You do, too."

"Who cares about tests? If we pull this off, we'll be legends."

"I don't want to be a legend. I want to sleep."

"You say that now, but think of the glory."

"Go to sleep," he said.

"Sleep is boring."

"*Sleep*," he groaned, burying his head beneath his pillow.

I thought of shaking him again, but I didn't want to piss him off. After standing by my bed for a moment, I decided to proceed without him. I pulled on my shirt and slipped out, already composing the story I'd get to tell Dickie and Heinous in the morning.

Hassert stormed the commons the next afternoon, ordering everyone into his wing. He instituted a complete lockdown. I asked Mike, our RC, what was going on, but he just rubbed his bald spot and said, "No talking."

The other RCs in our dorm stood by the exits, and from their stern, somber expressions, I knew this couldn't be good.

Once all the guys in our dorm were rounded up, Hassert led us to his room. The RCs lived in deluxe suites at the end of each wing. Hassert's room had this tribal decoration theme going on, with African carvings and colorful weavings hung on the walls. The place reeked of chicken soup. Hassert pointed to a nasty-looking brown bubble in the ceiling that dripped cloudy water into one of three buckets he'd arranged below. The pizza burrito I'd eaten for lunch started to creep up my throat.

Apparently, some "idiot joker" had propped a garbage can full of water and ramen noodles against Steve Lacone and Steve Dennon's door the night before. When the Steves had opened their door that morning, thirty gallons of chicken-flavored water had flooded their room. In itself, that might not have been such a huge deal, except the Steves lived on the second floor, directly above Hassert's apartment. Who knew?

"It's hard to believe," Hassert said, "that someone who goes to a school for so-called gifted students could do such an utterly stupid thing."

He drummed his fingers against the wooden door and looked straight at me. I tried my best to appear as surprised as everyone else.

"We're not leaving this hall until we get to the bottom of this," Hassert said. A hearty drop plunked into a bucket, splashing water on the orange-and-brown woven wall hanging. "Anyone care to explain who might have done such a stupid thing?"

His eyes scanned the students gathered in the hallway. Dickie and Heinous stood nearby, but I knew better than to look at them. Dickie hadn't even seemed that impressed by the prank. "That's nasty," was all he'd said that morning, when I'd told him about my late-night adventure.

"We'll wait here all day until someone speaks up," Hassert said.

I swallowed and stared at the buckets.

Drip.

Drip.

A few students groaned and sat with their backs against the wall.

"We'll stay through dinner if we need to," Hassert continued. "I don't care. I've got all the time in the world."

I leaned against the wall and considered my situation. Dickie wouldn't crack, and the only other person I'd told was Heinous. Maybe I was in the clear, but something else bothered me. The Steves? No. They might be our enemies, but they had their pride. They wouldn't go to Hassert.

I ran through the events of the night before. It had been a relatively simple matter to attach one of the custodian's hoses to the laundry room sink and fill the garbage can that I'd propped against the Steves' door. The tricky part was keeping everything quiet so I didn't wake the Steves before the prank was ready. Once the can had filled, I dumped in twelve packets of ramen, and voilà!— the great chicken flood was set. No one saw me, except when I returned the hose to the custodian's closet, I passed a person sitting in a patch of light by the stairwell.

At the time, I hadn't worried about it. He was just

another computer nerd whose roommate must have gotten fed up with his late-night pencil scratching, so he'd been kicked out into the hall to finish his homework. He hadn't said anything to me. Why would he care what I was doing? Guys like him lived in a separate world where the only things that mattered were virtual weapons specs and computer processor speeds.

Of course he'd seen me. And given that I'd been carrying a dripping hose at quarter past one, he must have known I was up to something. I tried to piece together his face—pale, skinny, with a mop of greasy hair and a pointy nose. *Muppet.*

I spotted Muppet sitting ten or so people down. He didn't look at me.

"I'm waiting," Hassert said.

Heinous raised his hand and my stomach knotted. Was he going to blow me in? Get rid of me so he could room with Dickie?

"What?" Hassert grumbled.

"Can we get our homework?" Heinous asked. "I have an English paper due tomorrow."

"No. No one's going anywhere."

"What if I have to go to the bathroom?" Heinous asked, contorting his face as if he couldn't hold it anymore.

"The next person who talks better have something to say about this . . . this vandalism, or they'll get a detention," Hassert said. "We'll stay here, gentlemen, for as long as it takes."

I looked at Muppet again. I'd never even called him by his real name. Ralph, maybe? Who could blame him if he told on me? There'd be one less jerk to make fun of him.

The pizza burrito threatened to come back up again. If Muppet said anything, I'd be expelled for sure. Maybe that's what I wanted, I thought. Maybe that's why I kept doing stupid things. Chuck could be right — this was just one more attempt to run away.

I watched the buckets fill.

Drip.

Drip.

Drip.

Magnets

EVERYONE STAYED IN THE HALL, complaining about how hungry they were and how they had to go to the bathroom or do homework. Ten minutes before the cafeteria closed, the RCs finally broke down and let us go. Apparently, they didn't have the authority to withhold food from us.

I kept waiting for the ax to fall. In the days that followed, Hassert made all the threats he could, revoked all the dorm privileges he was able to, and cornered everyone he thought might know something, but no one blew me in. Almost a week passed and I was still there. Every day I didn't get the call to start packing felt like borrowed time.

I used to imagine that if I only had a few weeks left to live, I'd do all sorts of crazy things like swim with sharks and skydive naked over Chicago. Only now that my life at ASMA really might be over, I didn't feel like doing anything crazy. Instead, I got serious about school. I behaved well in class and stayed up late doing homework. I even tried to get ahead on my physics group work, except I couldn't get very far with it.

The problem set Dr. Choi had given my group covered magnetism and electromagnetic fields. On a mathematical level, I knew the equations for calculating ohms, amps, volts, flux lines, and all that stuff. I could determine the strength of an electromagnet created by 12 volts run through a 2-ohm solenoid, and I could figure out exactly how much electricity would be induced by moving a 5-gauss magnet around a 1-centimeter iron pole at 3 rotations per second. But I couldn't explain *why* any of this worked.

According to Dr. Choi, magnetism was one of the fundamental forces of the universe. It determined everything from particle physics to the basic chemical bonds that held molecules together and resulted in life. It was essential. Yet not even Dr. Choi could tell me *why* opposite charges would attract and like charges repel. After all, when two different magnets were pulled together or pushed apart, what exactly went between them? What exerted the force? "That's how it goes," was all Dr. Choi said. "One of life's mysteries."

My physics group agreed to meet on the balcony above the main commons of the boys' dorm to finish the problem set. We'd never met as a group outside of class before, and the prospect of spending a couple hours studying with Ellie had me all mixed up. It was like the attraction and repulsion of magnets. On the one hand, I couldn't stop thinking about the glimpse of Ellie I'd gotten outside of Chuck's office. I even felt a little bad for her, because I figured that beneath the confident facade she might feel alone. But on the other hand, I couldn't stand how stuck-up and superior she acted, and how she treated me like I was no one.

I headed to the balcony ten minutes early. Ellie wasn't going to catch me blank-faced and tongue-tied this time. I envisioned myself in the pose of a misunderstood genius, chewing on the end of my pencil with a lock of purple hair draped over my eye while I worked on a problem set—too deep in thought to bother looking up when she arrived.

At least that was my plan, but when I got to the balcony, Muppet was already sprawled on the floor, papers scattered around him. He was hunched over his book, punching numbers into his graphing calculator. I glared. Hanging out with Muppet didn't fit the scene I'd had in mind. The air smelled a little funky, too, like wet tennis shoes. No. Bad James. After what Muppet had done for me, I shouldn't make fun of him.

"Hi, Ralph," I said.

He squinted at me. The thought that Ralph wasn't his real name crossed my mind, but he didn't correct me on it.

"What's up?" I asked.

"The ceiling," he replied. "Cumulus clouds. Stratosphere. Although *up* is a relative term."

"Uh . . . right," I said.

Ralph kept squinting at me.

"So," I continued, lowering my voice, "I wanted to ask you something about the other day. You know, when Hassert was grilling us."

"Because you flooded his room?" Ralph asked, dashing any hope I'd had that he hadn't recognized me.

I nodded. "Why didn't you tell on me?"

"I don't tattle," Ralph replied.

"You're not going to say anything to Hassert?"

"No."

"Why not?"

"Because you're in our group."

"What group?"

"Physics group." He gestured to the problem set he was working on. "You can't go."

"What do you care?" I asked.

"Because we're friends."

It felt like a bowling ball had been tossed into my gut. My legs grew weak and I slid to the ground, sitting with my back against the balcony wall. Why Muppet, I mean Ralph, would think of us as friends was beyond me. "I'm not a very good friend."

"I know," he said. "Regardless, I'd miss you."

"You would?"

"Uh-huh. So don't get kicked out. Okay?"

"Okay."

He thrust his hand toward me. I stared at it, not sure what he wanted.

Ralph took my hand and gave it a shake. Then he hunched over his calculator and went back to punching in numbers.

Cheese and Ellie arrived a few minutes later. Ellie had on baggy pajama bottoms and a loose sweatshirt. Nonetheless, she managed to look like she was going to a photo shoot instead of a physics study session with guys whose biggest thrill was finding equations that made their graphing calculators draw breasts. She laughed at something Cheese said and nudged his shoulder.

"What's up?" My voice cracked.

"Hey," Cheese said.

Ellie didn't say anything. She was all business while we studied. She worked with Cheese on one half of the problem set while Ralph and I were supposed to do the other. I tried horsing around to lighten the mood—stealing a sheet of paper that she was using, folding it into an airplane, and launching it off the balcony, but she ignored me and wrote out her solutions on a new page.

After the first hour, we decided to order pizza. Everyone chipped in, and Ellie actually spoke to me. She said, "No onions," then went back to working with Cheese. I don't know why she bothered telling me anything, because when the pizza arrived, she barely ate any of it. She just picked at the crust and sipped her Diet Coke.

I didn't eat much either. The stomach-go-flip feeling I got whenever Ellie was around wouldn't go away.

"Are any of you going to the Spring Fling?" she asked.

The dance was still over a month away, but everyone considered it a big deal. The only time girls at ASMA dressed up in high heels and slinky dresses was for the fling. Guys were supposed to dress up, too, but they usually looked worse in tuxes than they normally did.

"I'm going," Ralph said. "I have a date."

Coke almost came out my nose. "Who?"

"She's not from this school," Ralph said, scratching behind his ear. "She's a girl from a different school, but I checked the rule book and that's allowed."

"An import," Cheese said. "You sly dog."

Ralph blushed. "Na-uh. She's American."

Cheese and I chuckled.

"What about you, Cheese?" Ellie asked.

He licked some pizza sauce off his fingers and reached for another slice. "I don't know."

"Beth Lindbergh," I prodded. "She's into you."

Cheese hunched his shoulders. "Maybe. But I like more zaftig girls."

"Zaftig?" I asked.

"You never heard of zaftig?" Cheese replied. "That's my favorite word, man. It means big boobs."

"No way."

"Look it up."

"You want to know my favorite word?" Ellie said. "It's a science word."

"Ah, science," I mocked. "The language of love."

"I'm serious."

My heart skipped at the thought that we were actually almost having a conversation. "So what's the word?"

"*Syzygy.*"

Cheese and I glanced at each other. Ralph spilled a gob of sauce down his shirt.

"It means," she explained, "a kind of unity or conjunction. Like in psychology, Jung used *syzygy* to describe the total wholeness that happens when the masculine and feminine come together. And in astronomy, syzygy is when celestial bodies are arranged in a straight line, as in an eclipse." She brushed a lock of hair out of her eyes and tucked it behind her ear. "So when you think about all the different meanings, syzygy is like connecting with someone in a celestial way. Pretty, huh?"

"Yeah," I squeaked, my voice breaking again.

Cheese cracked a goofy smile. "What about a conjunction of zaftig bodies, like with me in the middle? Zaftig syzygy."

"You're such a perv," Ellie said, smacking his shoulder.

It made my chest ache to see how comfortable she was with him.

"How about you?" she asked Ralph. "What's your favorite word?"

Ralph swallowed a bite of pizza and wiped his mouth on his sleeve. "Pi."

"Like the pie you eat?" Ellie asked.

"Or hair pie?" Cheese asked.

"Or cow pie?" I asked.

"No, no, no," Ralph replied. "The *number* pi. Duh."

I had to hand it to Ralph—he was original. "That's not even a word," I teased.

"I just said it, didn't I?"

"He's got you there," Cheese said. "Mmmm . . . pie."

"Okay, how do you spell it?"

Ralph typed something into his calculator, then held it out for me to see. 3.14159.

"Wow," I said, trying to joke with him. "You could win the nerd spelling bee."

Ellie gave me an icy look. "I like pi," she told Ralph. Then she went back to talking with Cheese about who he could take to the fling.

I grew quiet after that. She'd asked everyone for their favorite word except me.

By the time we finished the problem set, there was only half an hour left before curfew. Cheese and Ralph went to the computer room, and Ellie headed for her dorm.

I followed her out. It was probably a dumb thing to do, but I couldn't stand how she kept acting like I didn't exist. "Don't you want to know my favorite word?" I called.

Ellie slowed. "Sure."

My skin prickled as I caught up to her. We were almost exactly the same height. "*Ucalegon*," I said, stretching the word out.

She smiled. "That's pretty. It sounds like whales swimming. What's it mean?"

"A neighbor whose house is on fire."

"Figures. I should have known you'd pick something like that." She slung her backpack over her shoulder and continued toward her dorm.

I walked after her. It was a cold night, so there weren't many people out. Ellie had a coat on, but I didn't. Still, my face felt hot and flushed. "Hey!" I said. "Why do you hate me so much?"

"I don't hate you." She kept walking, stepping around a puddle. Most of the snow and ice from winter had melted, leaving the ground muddy. "I just don't like it when people show off."

"I don't show off."

"Yes, you do. You're always trying to impress people."

I considered this for a moment. "Is that why you ditched me—the night I jumped in the pond?"

"I didn't think you'd actually do that," Ellie admitted. "Sometimes guys do crazy things when I'm around, so I figured if I wasn't around, you wouldn't do anything."

"I'm pretty good at being crazy on my own."

She laughed.

"What's so funny?" I asked.

"You." She headed to a bench and sat, crossing her legs. "You act so intimidating."

"Me?" I scoffed, sitting beside her. "You're the intimidating one."

"No, I'm not."

"Yes, you are. Miss Perfect in every way."

I meant it as a compliment, but Ellie's smile fell. She stared at the ground.

"What did I do now?"

"I hate that," she said. "*Perfect.* Why does everyone expect me to be perfect?"

"I'm not saying you have to be perfect. You just are."

"Trust me: I'm not."

I remembered how scared she'd looked when I'd seen her outside Chuck's office. "I didn't tell anyone," I said. "You know—about you meeting with Chuck. Not that it's a big deal. Lots of people see him."

"Do you?" she asked.

"I only went because of a friend."

"Oh."

"I probably won't go back," I added.

"That's too bad. Chuck's a good person. If it weren't for him, I probably wouldn't have anyone to talk to."

"Hold up. You've got more friends than anyone."

She gave me a perplexed look.

"You're always dating someone," I said.

Ellie smirked. "Guys never fall for me. They only fall for their idea of me."

"Well, what about your other friends?"

"You mean the ones who keep adding comments to my site?"

"Huh?"

"Don't tell me you don't know about it."

"I don't."

Ellie sighed. "About a week after you jumped in the pond, someone put up a site about me. The address is 'Pond Skank,' but the pictures are all me. There's even a nifty drawing of me, rising out of the pond like the Lady of the Lake, waiting to 'skankify' guys."

"You're kidding."

"I wish," she replied. "According to the site, my hobbies include luring guys into the pond with my skanky charms and getting them expelled. Or, in your case, suspended. Although there's speculation that I poisoned you and threw you into the pond myself, hoping you'd drown."

"Ouch."

"It's very amusing," she said. "You should see all the clever remarks people have left about me."

"Why don't you have it taken down?"

"What's the point? People would still hate me."

"No, they wouldn't."

Ellie shook her head. "I know what people say about me. They think I'm stuck-up. Even before the pond incident, they called me the Ice Queen."

I glanced away, wondering if she knew that I was one of those people. "What about Amber Lane, or Jewel

Sens, or Brandy Morales?" I asked. "They practically worship you."

"They probably started the site."

"That sucks."

"I'm used to it. All my life, people have been nice to my face, then they cut me apart behind my back. No one's ever straight with me."

"I'll be straight with you," I said, hoping I didn't sound too cheesy.

"Yeah, right."

"I will," I said. "How about this—I always thought you were stuck-up."

"Good to know."

"But you're not stuck-up," I added. "Not really. It's just that most people are scared of you."

Ellie chuckled and her knee fell against mine. "Most people are scared of *you*, James."

"Are you scared of me?"

"A little."

"Why? It's not like I'm a gun-toting psycho."

"That isn't what scares me," she said. "It's more like I'm scared *for* you."

I glanced at my arm. A few of my scars were visible beyond the hem of my sleeve, but most were covered. "I can't believe this," I said, changing the subject. "We're talking. I mean, really talking. I feel like I know you."

"Maybe you do." She looked down, as if waiting for me to say something important.

"So are you . . . ?" I started, then my voice got lost in my throat. I swallowed and tried again. "Are you going to the fling with anyone?"

Ellie seemed taken aback by my question. "Oh," she said. "Kevin Heegan asked me."

"Really?" Heegan was a tall, buff junior with a perfectly square jaw. All the excitement I'd felt the moment before drained out of me. It was like in movies when the bad guy blew a hole through the side of a plane and everything got sucked into the empty sky.

"I haven't told him if I'm going or not," she added. "I was kind of hoping someone else might ask. What about you?"

"I don't know. There are a few people I could ask."

"Like who?"

"Jessica Keen, for one."

"Didn't you two break up?"

"We had a little disagreement," I said. "She probably expects me to ask her, but I haven't talked with her since she got all weird and possessive over Christmas break."

"That's not what I heard."

"Whatever." I glanced away. Heegan. I couldn't believe she'd go with Heegan. I guess he fit the part by being appropriately hunkish. "Look, I'll tell you what really happened with Jess, but you have to keep it a secret. Okay?"

Ellie nodded.

"The truth is, these guys were chasing us, and I could have fought them, but I didn't want to. Not with Jess there. So I tried to get away, and we got in an accident, and she flipped out."

"Someone was chasing you?"

"These guys who wanted to fight me. I used to be in a street-fighting league, and I was never defeated."

"See? That's what I'm talking about," Ellie said. "Why are you always telling stories?"

"It's not a story." I rolled up my sleeve and showed her the scars on the inside of my arm. "That's how I got these."

Ellie dragged her finger over my scars. For a moment, I thought I had her, but when she spoke, it was in a hard, cold voice. "God, James. You don't have to lie."

"I'm not lying."

"That's right," she said, "you're all car crashes, and explosions, and fights to the death. A real hero."

I jerked my sleeve down. "Forget it."

"Forget what?"

"You are stuck-up," I said. Attraction. Repulsion. "You want to know why people hate you? It's not because you're pretty. It's because you're cold. You're so cold, you're dead inside."

Ellie's mouth tightened. Her eyes grew wet and tears rolled down her cheeks, which was strange, because other than the tears she didn't look like she was crying.

I stood. More tears rolled down her cheeks. I wanted to take it back, but I couldn't. So instead, I walked away.

GOnE

johnnyrotten: Hey, I saw you blip on. I have to ask you something.

ghost44: What?

johnnyrotten: I want to ask you a question, but before you answer you have to let me explain. Okay?

ghost44: I need to go.

johnnyrotten: Just give me one minute.

ghost44: Fifty-six seconds left.

johnnyrotten: Will you go to the dance with me?

johnnyrotten: Don't answer yet!

johnnyrotten: Here's the thing. I know you think that if I see you, it'll ruin everything, but I promise it won't. You're the only person I can talk with, and that's more important than appearances—I get that now. I swear, how you look doesn't matter to me. If you want, I'll even wear a blindfold all night. It'll be like a blind date and we can be with each other.

ghost44: You are so pathetic. I can't believe I ever wrote you.

johnnyrotten: What's wrong?

ghost44: God, I'm such an idiot. I took your stupid advice. I tried reaching out. I tried to believe that things might be different with you—that there might be something honest in you, but I was wrong.

johnnyrotten: What do you mean?

ghost44: You're the one who's cold, James. You're the one who's dead inside.

johnnyrotten: Ellie?

ghost44: Don't ever IM me again.

johnnyrotten: Wait!

johnnyrotten: I'm sorry.

johnnyrotten: Come on, Ellie. Talk to me.

johnnyrotten: Please.

johnnyrotten: Ellie?

johnnyrotten: Are you there?

M^uck

I SHOULD HAVE CRIED, but I couldn't. Not one damn tear. It didn't matter that I'd lost everything—Jess, Ellie, ghost44—I felt nothing. *I* was dead inside. A cold, dead shell pretending to be human, while everyone else took it for granted that they were real. They didn't have to lie all the time. They didn't have to cut themselves to feel.

I locked the door and slugged cough syrup until my stomach burned. Dickie was out, probably hanging in Cheese and Heinous's room. I unplugged my alarm and stuffed some earplugs in so I wouldn't hear him when he returned. Then I collapsed onto my bed, wanting to lose myself in sleep.

Almost as soon as I closed my eyes, I fell through the mattress into the dark, cloudy night of the city.

I dreamed of a courtyard surrounded on all four sides by brick buildings. The Thief was there, kneeling at the base of a scraggly tree. She poured water from a cup into cracks where the gnarled roots pushed up slabs of concrete. "It's dying," she said. "Every day it loses more leaves."

I looked at the tree. A few leaves clung to one branch near the top, but the rest were bare. "Can you help me?" I asked.

The Thief kept tending the tree, holding the cup upside down until the last drops dripped onto the roots.

"Please," I added. "I need to find a way out of here."

She shook her head and set the cup down. "You can't leave."

"Why not?"

The Thief gazed at the brick walls surrounding us. "The buildings have grown so tall, they block out the light," she said. "I can bring the tree water, but I can't bring it light. Time's running out, James. When the tree dies, you'll forget this place."

"Good. I want to forget it. I don't want to be here anymore."

"You don't understand." Her eyes locked on mine. "Part of you will always be here. You simply won't remember what you've left behind anymore. You won't remember that you once were someone different."

I realized she was talking about White Blade. She knew what I'd done to him—how I'd helped the Nomanchulators take him.

"I warned you not to go after him," she said. "But you wanted to take control. Rewrite your life. You gave yourself to them—that's why you're trapped here."

"What if I rescued him?" I asked.

She seemed surprised by the idea. "I thought you wanted to get rid of him."

"I did."

"Then what changed?"

A breeze swirled dry leaves around the courtyard. "I'm becoming like them," I said. "Like the Nomanchulators. If I undo what I've done, I'll be able to leave, right?"

"Perhaps."

"So all we have to do is find where the Nomanchulators took White Blade and take him back."

The Thief sighed and shook her head. "It's not that easy."

"Why not? You're the Thief—isn't that what you do? Steal things?"

"What the Nomanchulators take, they drag to the core," she explained. "Even if we could make it down there, it would be near impossible to free him."

"Please," I said. "I don't want to stay like this."

She looked at the bare branches above her, then back at me. "If we go down there, we might not make it out."

"Things can't get any worse," I said.

"Things can always get worse," she replied.

On the way to the elevator, the Thief explained what we had to do. The core existed several levels beneath the burrows. "Remember the first time you went to the burrows?"

I nodded as if it was no big deal, even though I'd gotten the crap kicked out of me.

"This is going to be like that, only harder. The deeper we go, the less you'll be able to control."

"Fine."

"Things will change," continued the Thief. "Not much can stay solid in the core. It's possible you'll forget yourself and never return." She looked at me to see if I understood what we were getting into. "Are you sure you want to do this?"

"What other choice do I have?" I said, pushing the button to call the elevator. The brass doors opened, and I stepped inside.

"All right," the Thief said, sitting on the bed beside me. "The important thing is to remember how many levels you go down."

I lay on the bed and closed my eyes. It took several minutes before I drifted off and the elevator started to descend. The tarnished brass walls glistened with the oil-on-water sheen of the burrows. Even the Thief appeared brighter, her blue eyes impossibly intense.

"One," I said.

"No. This is two. You have to count the surface as one, because from where we are now, you'd need to wake up twice to make it out."

"Right," I replied, embarrassed to have made such an obvious mistake. "Two."

I folded my hands across my chest and closed my eyes to dream of the next level. Sleep came quickly—a sudden drop that ended with a ding! The old-fashioned arrow above the door rotated back a notch.

"Three."

My voice sounded funny. Disconnected. There was a lag between the movement of my lips and when I heard myself speak. The Thief leaned over me. "You're doing fine," she said, her mouth moving out of sync with her words. "Focus on the elevator. Keep going."

I took a deep breath and closed my eyes again. This time it was like the brakes on the elevator had snapped. I fell for a long time before I woke in the next level. The brass walls swirled with color, and the bed I lay on undulated when I moved. I rubbed my eyes. The bones of my arm flexed and wobbled.

I sat up, terrified. My elbow bumped the wall, sending ripples through the whole elevator. Nothing here, not even myself, was solid.

"Easy," the Thief said. Her eyes drifted around, making me seasick.

"How much farther?"

"As far as you can go."

I swallowed and lay on the swaying bed. The elevator lurched back and forth for what seemed like hours before I fell asleep again and dropped to the next level.

Where was I?

An elevator—that much I remembered. But there was something else I'd forgotten. Something important. "Four," I said, recalling my purpose. "No. Five."

I looked at the old-fashioned dial above the brass doors for confirmation. The arrow had melted. It dripped down the wall like candle wax.

Everything began to melt. I held my hand in front of me and watched my fingers wilt and stretch like taffy in the hot sun. My mouth dropped open to scream, but my jaw wouldn't work.

"Focussss," murmured the Thief. She slouched on the bed, her head lolling off, melting from the heat of a brilliant spark within her chest. "Pullll-ittt-tooogether."

I nodded and tried to remember her face the

way it should be—her sharp cheekbones, wide smile, and intense eyes. Next, I willed my hand to be solid. My fingers drew back to their normal size. I flexed them a few times, head throbbing from the strain of it. The Thief held her palm to my cheek, as if checking my temperature. "Keep going," she said, helping me lie back.

I closed my eyes again and sought out sleep.

When next I dreamed, things looked translucent. The walls of the elevator were soap-bubble thin, and the Thief appeared ghostly and beautiful. The glow in her center that I'd seen before looked incredible—a radiant snowflake, twinkling and unique. I didn't want to see her solid anymore. I wanted both of us to be light and colors swirling around. The elevator dissolved, but I didn't care. I slipped free of my heavy, torpid self.

"James," came a whisper. It wasn't like a spoken word so much as a thought. "James, come back."

Come back to where? *I wondered.* There was no place. No time. We could go anywhere, quick as thought. Except I already was going somewhere. Sinking. How could I be sinking if I felt so light?

The elevator!

I tried to remember the walls. A shimmering bubble glistened around me. "You have to keep going," the Thief whispered. "Remember your purpose."

I yearned to keep the sense of airy freedom,

but part of me knew that if I stayed here, I might never wake up. "Six," I said, closing my eyes.

We fell through the ghost level and landed with a viscous splash. The elevator completely disappeared. Thick air, heavy with the swampy smell of decay, clogged my lungs. I stood, and my feet sank beyond my ankles into the cold, black muck. Without asking, I knew we'd reached the core.

I lurched forward, struggling to pull my legs out. The Thief gave me a hand, and my feet slurped loose, one at a time.

We were in a cave. Jars stacked on shelves hewn into the rough stone cast an orange glow throughout the room. There were hundreds of jars, each one containing a small, flickering entity that tinked against the glass like a trapped lightning bug.

"There," she said, pointing to a dark mass in the center of the cave. A web of cords radiated from the mass to the outer walls. "That's where they would have taken him."

The Thief hurried to the shelves on the outer walls, grabbing jars and placing them in a sack. I approached the dark mass in the middle. A shiny pod, taller than me, hung in the center like a giant translucent pumpkin seed suspended by a network of viney cords. I ducked beneath the cords to get a closer look.

At first, I could only make out a hand floating

inside the pod. Then a limp arm, crossing over a bent leg, the knee drawn up to the chest. His head was tilted forward, and his eyes were closed as though he were asleep. I recognized every detail of his face, from the freckle on his left cheek to the unevenly cut hair to the fine eyelashes on his shut eyes. It was me, only I'd never seen myself like this before—never with my eyes closed. I moved, half expecting this other to move with me, but it wasn't a mirror.

Who was I if I was watching myself sleep? *I thought.* Was I a dream of this sleeping self? Or was this other self my dream?

I reached to wake him, and my fingers pierced the outer shell, sinking into the warm, sticky fluid.

"We have to go," the Thief called.

Her voice startled me. I jerked my hand back, but the outer shell had closed around my wrist. I tried to pry my arm out, only my other hand got stuck as well. My legs had already sunk in up to my knees. A spasm of terror coursed through me. I pictured myself sinking until the muck filled my open mouth and sealed my lungs.

I heaved my arms back, shaking the seed. Strands from the web waved about, sticking to my cheeks and neck. The more I struggled, the more entangled I became.

"Stop!" The Thief set down her sack of jars and hurried to my side. "Look!" She pointed at a few of the cords that stretched to the ceiling. "They'll feel you. They'll come."

I quit struggling. Cold muck crept up my thigh.

"You have to stay calm," she said. Then she wrapped her arms around my chest and pulled.

Both my arms slid out to my wrists. I threw all my strength into it, yanking my left hand free. The pod shook, sending vibrations up the cords. Inside the pod, my other floated about like a corpse in water.

The Thief grabbed my right arm and pulled. It wasn't until my hand snapped free that I noticed her leg braced against the pod. Her foot had sunk in beyond her ankle.

She tore the sticky strands off me, and I fell free of the web. Muck splashed around my waist. That's when I spotted the Nomanchulators, emerging through dozens of holes in the domed ceiling.

A drone like a million locusts filled the chamber. Nomanchulators crawled down along the cords in a sickening swarm. The Thief craned her head to look at me. Strands stuck to her lips and cheeks. "Go!" she yelled. "Now!"

I reached for her, but she didn't bother to raise her hand. She hung from the sticky cords, limp as bait.

I tore out of that level the moment she started to scream.

Then silence. I was in the ghost level again—the

one of light and freedom. Through the transparent
walls of the elevator, I watched a long, dark shadow
stretch closer. Insect limbs probed the surface,
and a claw pushed against the bubble walls. The
Nomanchulators were coming, following me out.

Instinct told me to run, but I knew that
wouldn't help. I forced myself to concentrate on
waking to the next level.

My eyes snapped open. All around me the
walls melted. Sick, wet thuds shook the elevator
as the Nomanchulators scrabbled to get in. I woke
three more times in quick succession, like a diver
fighting to reach the surface before my air ran out.
My head reeled from the sudden changes until, at
last, the elevator appeared normal.

The walls, my face, the bed—all felt solid.
I tried to stand, but it took a moment before my
body moved. Something wasn't right. I shouldn't
be in an elevator, *I thought. It wasn't normal to*
fall asleep in an elevator. The deadening buzz of
the Nomanchulators grew louder.

I forced myself to wake again.

Dark.

Touching my face, I had to pry my eyelids apart. Then
I blinked against the brightness. A bird chirped, and rosy
light blazed through the window.

Morning had never looked so good.

FLighT

MY CLOCK SAID IT WAS ALMOST seven thirty. I skipped showering, threw on some clothes, grabbed my backpack, and hurried to class before I missed first period.

Chemistry. Ms. Krup was finishing with attendance when I scrambled in and took my seat. My stomach rumbled. During break I'd try to get something from the snack machine to make up for missing breakfast.

I drew a deep breath, relieved to have escaped the Nomanchulators. Being awake gave me a new appreciation for ordinary things—the fact that my desk was solid and the walls weren't melting and my hand would move when I told it to. All good.

Ms. Krup droned on and on about stoichiometry. Everyone around me scribbled notes, but I didn't get what people were writing down. The whole concept seemed too simple. You'd think, with a name like "stoichiometry," it would be something complicated and earth-shattering, except it wasn't.

Halfway through the lecture, someone knocked on the classroom door. Ms. Krup went over the same chemical reaction for the third time, pointing to the board with a bamboo stick as she approached the door. She glanced out the narrow window.

"Good," she said. "They're here."

Everyone set down their pencils.

A sense of dread filled me. I worried that whoever was knocking on the door might have come for me. Could it be Principal Durn? Or Hassert? I tried to remember what I could be in trouble for. I hadn't arrived that late, had I? Or was it because of the ramen incident? Had someone finally told on me?

I raised my hand. "Ms. Krup," I said, "please don't let them in."

She looked at me and frowned.

I felt ridiculous. It was probably only a guest lecturer or something. No one else in the classroom seemed concerned.

"Don't worry, James," Ms. Krup said. "It will all be over soon."

She turned the doorknob.

A wave of Nomanchulators flooded in, flattening Ms. Krup beneath their long insect legs. I scrambled to the back of the room, but there were no other exits. All the students stood and turned to face me. Their eyes and mouths had been stitched shut.

I yelled and kicked the wall, desperate to get out. It was no use. I had to maintain control. Think. This must be a dream, and if it was a dream, I could wake up.

My heart skipped as a Nomanchulator reached for me. I ducked its arm and lurched back, hitting the wall. A dull, metallic smell flooded my lungs. More Nomanchulators crowded the room, numbing my bones with their chittering. I grabbed a pencil off my desk and jabbed the point into my hand.

Pain surged up my arm, ripping me out of the dream.

I lurched upright in bed. My hand hurt. Glancing around, I tried to determine if I really was awake or if this could be another trick. The shades were drawn, and things looked dull. I touched the wall—it felt solid enough. How many levels had I come up? Seven? Or six? My clock was blank, which seemed strange.

Angry thuds pounded the door. I slid out of bed. Someone pounded again, shaking the door in its metal frame, only the sound was muffled. Unreal. I pinched my arm and slapped my cheeks.

The pounding quickened.

I hurried to the window and raised the shade. If this was level one, I'd be able to fly away until my alarm went off and pulled me from the dream. I grabbed a chair and threw it at the glass. It bounced off. Weird. I swung the chair again, putting more force into it.

The window shattered into hundreds of glistening triangles. For an instant, all was quiet, then the Nomanchulators pounded the door again. I climbed onto the window ledge, jumping just as the door burst open.

Cool air rushed past me. Reaching out with my mind, I tried to bend things so I could fly, yet my body kept falling.

I hit the ground with a jolt that punched the wind out of my chest.

It hurt more than it ever had in a dream. I'd only fallen twelve or so feet, but I'd landed on broken glass. My shoulder and thigh stung. Coughs wracked my body as I struggled to draw breath back into my empty lungs.

An RC ran across the field toward me. I realized that I wasn't wearing a shirt. The morning dew chilled my chest, while other parts of me burned with pain. A few shards of glass seemed to be lodged in my palm.

"Holy shit!" Heinous said. He and Dickie leaned out the broken window above.

The earplugs had come out, making things sound real again. Someone shouted my name, asking if I was okay. A crowd gathered. From the window, Heinous erupted into surprised, hysterical laughter.

Automatism

THE SCHOOL NURSE CLEANED ME UP. Some of the cuts were long, but most weren't very deep, so I didn't need stitches. "You're going to have some impressive scars," she said.

Hassert didn't waste any time scheduling my expulsion hearing for the next day. As soon as I got back to my dorm, I found out about it. Everything was arranged very formally. Instead of meeting in Principal Durn's office, we were meeting in the Conference Chambers—a fancy room on the second floor with a big table where the school board gathered.

My dad had to take off work to attend. I greeted my parents in front of the school. Dad wore his normal wrinkled white work shirt with a brown checkered tie. Moms, on the other hand, had obviously dressed up for the occasion—bright red blouse, black skirt, and a cloud of perfume hovering around her. She'd probably spent all morning getting herself ready, "putting on her face," as she called it.

"Are you okay?" Moms asked, worry lines creasing her cheeks.

"I'm fine," I said.

She and Dad looked at each other.

"Do you have much homework today?" Dad asked.

"I don't know. I'm missing physics class right now."

"Oh," he replied, as if only then remembering that it was the middle of the school day.

"I can't believe this, James," Moms said. "What's going on with you? Is it us? Did we do something?"

I didn't even try to address Moms's questions. It bothered me how she always made everything about herself. "The meeting starts at two o'clock," I said, glancing at my watch.

On the way to the Conference Chambers, I gave them a little tour. "My English classroom is down there," I said. "Those are some of our Beat poetry projects. Mine's the cube hanging from the ceiling. And the big goldfish in that tank is called Lucky because every year for Saint Patrick's Day someone dyes the water green. There used to be other fish, but they all died. Lucky eats Tater Tots."

My parents nodded, seeming interested. I guess I'd never told them much about ASMA before.

I took them upstairs and showed them the library, along with the view from the balcony.

"Is that clock right?" Dad asked. According to a clock on the wall, we were five minutes late.

"We're almost there," I said, leading them along the balcony to the Conference Chambers.

Linda opened the door and invited us in. My parents and I sat on one side of the long table. Everyone else was already seated.

Principal Durn made the introductions. Nancy Snodgrass, the Head Director, sat at the far end of the table, wearing a blazer with shoulder pads so big they made her look like a triangle. Mr. Funt was there, too, since he was the Sophomore Class Adviser, and Hassert, Head of Residential Life. Linda, who'd be taking "minutes" on our meeting, sat at the other end of the table next to Chuck.

Chuck didn't mention that I'd met him before. He looked different, although I couldn't put my finger on why. Maybe he'd shaved. Principal Durn introduced him as Dr. Charlie Rainen and said he was there as Director of Student Services. Everyone had their titles.

And then there was me. Head of Screwing Up. Insane Action Adviser. Director of Student Destruction—that's what Hassert might call me. But from Principal Durn's tired expression, I figured he'd give me a title like Chief Nuisance, or Waste of Opportunity.

Hassert began the meeting by reading his report on

"the incident." Apparently, when I hadn't shown up for breakfast, Heinous and Dickie had come back to the dorm to play a little drum solo on my door. Then they heard a loud noise, unlocked the door, and barged in. That's when I pulled my Superman and jumped out, or in Hassert's terms, "fled the scene of destruction."

Hassert went on to detail damage to the chair (the chair, for Christ's sake!) and how much window repairs would cost ($356!). He listed my previous three strikes— the ultimate freak incident in the cafeteria (which he called "a tasteless mock shooting"), the "profanity" scrawled on my forehead (EAT ME?), and the pond incident. In Hassert's lingo, my winter swim translated to "reckless behavior while under the influence of an illicit substance." Finally, he clarified that I was already on academic and disciplinary probation for my previous actions. He closed his manila folder and sat back, satisfied.

Principal Durn looked like he'd fallen asleep. His elbows were propped on the table and he held his forehead in his hands so his bald spot pointed directly at me.

"Was a drug test performed?" Ms. Snodgrass asked. I couldn't believe it—like smoking pot would make me jump out a window.

"Oh, God." Moms gasped. "Drugs? You think James is on drugs?"

"Please understand, Mrs. Turner: it's our policy in situations like this to consider all contributing factors."

"I wasn't *on* anything," I started to say, neglecting to mention the cough syrup.

Hassert cut me off. "Regrettably, no drug test was performed. The, uh, Resident Counselor on duty failed to make a proper substance-abuse assessment."

Ms. Snodgrass jotted something on her notepad. "Mr. and Mrs. Turner, I hope you understand that, from a legal standpoint, your son's behavior has become a liability to this institution. In addition, he's broken the terms of his enrollment contract."

"Excuse me," Chuck interrupted. "This isn't merely a *legal* issue. This young man's future is at stake."

The director gave Chuck a long look. I got the distinct sense that Chuck wasn't much liked by the administration. "Certainly," Ms. Snodgrass replied in a clipped voice. "Of course the well-being of the student is foremost on my mind. But as a public residential learning institution, we're not equipped to deal with these types of behavioral issues. If a student hurts himself or, God forbid, attempts suicide, we could be found negligent."

"I wasn't trying to kill myself," I said.

Principal Durn raised his head and focused his tired gaze on me. "Would you like to explain, James, what exactly you *were* trying to do?"

"Well," I began, "it was an accident."

Hassert scoffed. "So the chair *accidentally* flew through the window?"

"I thought I was asleep."

Principal Durn sighed. He rubbed his face, stretching his cheeks up around his eyes. "Never, in twenty years of being a principal, have I seen a student destroy school property and jump out a window *in his sleep.*" He drew a deep breath and stared at me, Director of Dumb-Ass Excuses. "James, it seems that these meetings have become a habit with you. I'm disappointed to see you here again. Disappointed, because you're smart enough to know better. Mr. Funt tells me you're a good student. You have strong grades. . . ."

Mr. Funt nodded. I felt bad about being rude to him before.

"But from where I sit," Principal Durn continued, "it looks like you're determined to get yourself kicked out. Frankly, I agree with Ms. Snodgrass." He turned to my parents. "I'm sorry, Mr. and Mrs. Turner, but I see no other choice than to discontinue your son's enrollment."

"Discontinue?" Moms asked. "You're saying he's going to be expelled?"

"I'm afraid so."

"It's the middle of the semester. Where do you expect him to go?"

"He can transfer back to his previous high school."

Moms and Principal Durn kept talking about my transcript and how this would affect my college admissions, but I stopped paying attention. I pictured myself back at my old school—the claustrophobic, dull-green hallways, burnt-out teachers, and students who thought I was nobody. I could't go back to that.

"Principal Durn," I interrupted. "Please let me stay. I'll be good."

"How do you expect us to believe you, given your behavior?" Principal Durn replied. "You've had warnings, James, and yet you've continued to break academy rules."

"I was asleep," I repeated. It sounded lame, even to me. No one spoke for several seconds, waiting for some other explanation, except I didn't have any other explanation. "I . . . I thought I was dreaming."

Hassert leaned forward, placing his doughy hands on the table. "You might think we're being hard on you, James," he said. "But what we're doing is for your own good. When young people aren't given consequences for their actions, they keep pushing the limits to test what they can get away with. I've seen it before. This time it might be jumping out a window. Next time overdosing on drugs, or driving a car into a tree." He shook his head, as if all this was very difficult for him. "Your behavior is getting increasingly reckless because you crave boundaries. I believe we have to expel you, otherwise you won't take your actions seriously."

Principal Durn checked his watch and shuffled some papers. "Anyone else have something to add?"

"Automatism," Chuck said.

Ms. Snodgrass scrunched her face, like she smelled something foul. "Care to clarify?"

"Sleepwalking. If James was asleep when the incident took place, we can hardly hold him accountable."

"I'm not buying that for a second," Hassert said.

"I suppose you're aware that five percent of all young males are sleepwalkers?" Chuck asked, focusing on Hassert. I finally realized why Chuck looked different— his glass eye was in. I couldn't even tell which one was fake.

"As someone in charge of Residential Life," he continued, "that's probably something you should know about. Although it's not usually violent, there are many cases where people have gotten dressed, left their homes, even driven cars while sleepwalking. I can refer you to the journal articles if you like."

Hassert frowned. "As interesting as such articles might be, I don't see what it's got to do with this."

"Really?" Chuck asked. "If you did a little research, you'd find that individuals have been acquitted of crimes, including murders, that were committed while sleepwalking. So if courts of law have found that someone can't be held accountable for actions committed while in a state of automatism, I don't see how we can be different." He turned to Ms. Snodgrass. "Legally speaking, that is."

Chuck's point suddenly hit me. If I was expelled, I could appeal it based on what he'd said. I wished Dickie was with me, flipping through his rule book.

"This is ridiculous," Hassert blurted out.

"And what explanation do you have for why someone would jump out a second-story window?" Chuck asked.

"He wants attention," Hassert said.

Chuck grinned. "Is that your *expert* opinion?"

"Gentlemen," Principal Durn said, cutting off Hassert's angry response. He cleared his throat and folded his hands. "What's your recommendation, Dr. Rainen?"

"Continued academic and disciplinary probation," Chuck said. "In addition, James will be required to see me on a biweekly basis until it's determined that he's psychologically stable and his sleepwalking episodes are appropriately treated."

Ms. Snodgrass shook her head. "You'd need parental consent, and a signed waiver to cover us for negligence."

"Mr. Turner and I have already spoken about this," Chuck replied.

"Mr. Turner?" Principal Durn asked.

My dad cleared his throat. "I agree with Charlie here. I'd like James to get some help."

Moms shook her head. "He doesn't need a shrink."

"James needs counseling," Chuck said. "And he needs our support."

"I'm sorry?" Moms replied. "Are you suggesting that I don't support my son? You'll excuse me if I'd prefer that my son not talk about his personal life with a total stranger."

"Hannah," Dad mumbled.

Moms threw up her hands. "You've no idea," she said to no one in particular. "I'm a good mother."

Principal Durn cleared his throat. "James, would you mind stepping into the hall for a few minutes?"

My chair screeched as I pushed back from the table. Moms wouldn't look at me. She searched through her purse for a tissue.

Linda shut the door.

I wandered the balcony that overlooked the central area of the school. The sounds of students talking and laughing below echoed up to me. Classes had ended for the day, so most of the building was empty except in one of the pits—these sunken amphitheaters with orange-carpeted stairs that formed seats—a bunch of students had gathered for Club Pseudo.

The club put on a variety show every Friday night. It was a combination of juggling club, bad drama, cheesy dances, garage bands, and strange eggs who didn't fit in any other club. Ralph and Jesus John were down there practicing their magic act. Both of them wore top hats and capes. The getup looked especially ridiculous on Ralph since his head was so small that the top hat kept falling over his eyes. And then there were the Buttles—a group of band geeks who wrote new lyrics for Beatles tunes. One was plucking out notes on a cheap synthesizer while three others appeared to be singing a version of "Piggies" involving biology class and dissecting fetal pigs. Behind them, two girls practiced a ribbon dance.

When I'd first come to ASMA, I'd sworn never to be a part of Club Pseudo. It was obviously deep in dork territory. Except now, looking out from the balcony, I liked it. Part of me wished I could be down there with them, although I didn't have any talents. Maybe I could join the Buttles and make up songs.

If I got kicked out, I'd miss it—not just hanging with Dickie, Heinous, and Cheese, or the pranks, or Ellie (even though she'd probably never talk to me again)—I'd miss Ralph and Club Pseudo. At my old school, if you sang a stupid song and did a ribbon dance, you'd get the shit kicked out of you. Here, people clapped.

This is a good place, I thought, recalling what Liam had said. It wasn't just the teachers or the fancy labs that made it good. It was that you could sit in a circle with a bunch of students and juggle bananas, sing, recite poetry, do a dance, whatever. The geeks had courage. They weren't afraid to be themselves.

Linda stuck her head out a few minutes later and called me back in.

Everyone in the meeting room, including my parents, looked solemn. I promised myself that if I got to stay, I'd go to Club Pseudo and clap my heart out for every act.

"Do you agree to the conditions set by Dr. Rainen?" Principal Durn asked.

It took me a moment to realize he meant Chuck. "Sure."

"You'll need to sign a contract. Your parents are going to sign one as well."

"We're going out on a limb for you," Ms. Snodgrass added. "I hope you recognize that."

"So I'm not getting kicked out or suspended?"

"There are no more suspensions for you," Principal Durn replied. "If you mess up again, you're expelled."

I tried my best to keep from smiling while the administrators gathered their papers.

Dad stood by the doorway, thanking Principal Durn and Ms. Snodgrass. Then he returned to the table and helped Moms stand. Her mascara had smeared, running into her wrinkles and making her face look old and bruised.

"I'll walk you to your car," I offered.

"No, no." Mom's voice shook a little. She turned her head and wiped her eyes with a tissue. I guess she'd been crying. "I don't know who you are anymore, James."

It surprised me how defeated she sounded. Moms had always seemed so monumental to me—like a planet with too much gravity that kept pulling me out of my orbit. Only now, it was as if I'd broken free, and I could finally see her for what she was—a fragile, lost person. "It's okay," I said. "I don't know who I am, either."

She frowned, then rifled through her purse for a mirror. Moms never liked anyone to see her when her makeup wasn't right.

Dad broke the silence. "You should get back to class. Keep up with your studies."

I gave them directions on how to find their way out of the building. Dad led Moms away, keeping his hand around her waist. I watched them go, realizing that maybe she needed him more than he needed her.

Chuck waited for me outside the conference room. "James, can I talk with you?" he asked once my parents had gone. "Just so you know, I don't think you were sleepwalking."

"You don't?"

"Nope."

"But you convinced them I was."

"I convinced them it was a possibility," he corrected. "To be honest, I agree with Mr. Hassert. Unless something happens, you'll end up dead." He gave me a long look.

"This is stupid. I really was asleep."

"That's my point. You don't see the danger you're in." Chuck put his thick hand on my shoulder. "Listen, James, you want to talk about stupid? I've known students who've killed themselves because they wanted to annoy their parents, or get back at the guy who dumped them, or impress their friends. They don't realize how much their lives are worth."

I tried to meet Chuck's stare, but I couldn't.

"That's the last time I'll cover for you," Chuck said. He squeezed my shoulder. "I'll see you Tuesday at two thirty.

If you're so much as a minute late, you might as well head straight to your dorm and pack your bags. Understand?"

"Yeah," I replied. Then I remembered that I'd meant to be angry at him for talking with my dad behind my back. "Hey, whatever happened to me making my own decision about coming to see you?"

"You did make a decision," he said. "You jumped out a window."

Part V

They say the

owl was a baker's daughter. Lord! we know

what we are, but not what we may be.

—*HAMLET,* ACT 4, SCENE 5

Normal

I DROPPED BY HEINOUS AND CHEESE'S room the day after my hearing. I figured that's where Dickie must be hanging out, since I hadn't seen him in a while.

Everyone grew quiet when I pushed open the door. Dickie was sitting on a desk, eating chips, while Heinous played a video game.

"Hey," Dickie said, looking concerned. "How's it going?"

"I wasn't kicked out," I replied.

"That's great! So you're not in trouble?"

"Nope," I said, leaving off the part about having to see Chuck twice a week.

"Wow. That must have been some sweet talking you did."

Heinous cursed at the video game and chucked the controller aside. "What's up, J.T.?"

"Not much."

There was an odd silence as, for once in his life, Heinous seemed unable to come up with anything else to say. I kind of wished he'd tease me—call me Smash or the Defenestrator or something—but he didn't.

"So did that guy come by our room to fix the window?" Dickie asked.

"Yeah. It's good as new."

"Cool."

"Sorry I laughed," Heinous said. "You know, when you jumped."

"Don't worry about it," I told him.

"It was just so crazy," he said. Then he looked at Dickie like he thought he'd said something wrong. "I mean, the whole scene, with the chair, and you not wearing a shirt or anything . . ."

"Really, don't worry about it," I repeated, but I could tell that something had shifted between us.

I'd crossed the line between acting strange and actually being strange.

Over the next week, I began to realize that it wasn't just with Dickie and Heinous that things had changed. In the hallways between classes, people literally looked away if I glanced at them, and when I entered a room, a low hiss of whispers would snuff out, as though people had been talking about how I'd tried to kill myself, or how I thought I was a bird, or whatever the latest theory was.

I'd become a popular subject of discussion, which was a far cry from being popular.

At Chuck's suggestion, I started running every day to blow off some steam. I kept to a strict schedule:

Wake at 6:30.

Shower.

Brush teeth.

Eat breakfast.

Attend classes.

Meet with Chuck (if a Chuck day).

More classes.

Return to my dorm.

Brush teeth.

Go for a run.

Do homework.

Eat dinner.

Brush teeth.

More homework.

Brush teeth.

Lights out.

Bed.

The schedule helped me keep things on an even keel. As long as I knew exactly what I was supposed to be doing, I didn't have time to get restless and mess up. Any free time I filled with brushing my teeth so I stayed minty fresh and in control.

Still, all work and no play made James a dull boy. Or rather, a very isolated, lonely boy. There were days when I barely spoke. I didn't even dream anymore—at least, not dreams that I remembered. In a way, it reminded me of how things had been at my old school. The main difference was that in the past, no one had bothered to talk with me because I was Mr. Invisible, the guy who didn't get an *H,* and now no one talked with me because I was Mr. Unstable, the guy who had jumped out a window.

More than ever, I missed ghost44, but every time I found her online, my messages were blocked.

Spring break came, which meant I had to go home. I survived the first few days holed up inside, watching TV and listening to music. Dad had to work, leaving Moms and me to avoid each other. She tried enticing me to go shopping again, only I'd learned my lesson from last time. I opted to stay on the couch and channel surf instead while she went out.

I watched so much TV, it was like I was an alien studying humanity through its broadcasts. Even lame "reality" shows about spring break fascinated me—all these greased-up Kens and Barbies laughing and dancing on the beach as if they couldn't imagine anything more fun. The kids on TV were supposed to be around my age, but none of them seemed remotely like me. I pictured myself strolling through the golden masses in my sport coat and ripped jeans, my purple hair spiked into a messy tangle. If I'd shown up at the beach, they probably would have kicked me off.

The more I watched, the lonelier I got. At the beginning

of the year, I'd wanted so badly to stand out, only now that I actually did stand out, I wanted to fit in—but I couldn't figure out how to do it. I couldn't even tell what was normal anymore. I suppose the teens on TV were meant to represent "normal" people, yet they weren't really normal at all. They were just what normal people were supposed to aspire to be—guys with buff chests and square jaws, and girls with perfect bodies, clear skin, and stylish hair. I'd never even met anyone who looked like them. Except Ellie.

If Ellie had strolled onto the *Spring Break Beach Party* set in a bikini, girls would have crumbled with envy and guys would have fallen all over themselves to talk with her. None of them would have gotten her, though. They wouldn't have understood when she talked about quantum mechanics, or the life of Emily Dickinson. They didn't know what *syzygy* meant.

Moms kept shopping, and I kept watching TV. Every day she came home with different tile samples and paint shades to redecorate the kitchen with. "I'm going for a Mediterranean look," she said. Then she grilled Dad and me on our opinions of various colors.

I tried to play along, yet I had trouble taking it seriously. Whatever color she chose to paint the walls, it wouldn't last. Moms changed the kitchen at least once a year. I used to think she did this to show off her "sophisticated sense of taste and style," but since the hearing I saw her differently. I even felt a little sad for her, because I knew that no matter what borders she used or how she tiled the backsplash, our kitchen would never be the kitchen she wanted.

Dad drove me to school Sunday night. He didn't talk much on the drive—not until we exited the highway and the lights of ASMA's campus glimmered above the cornfields.

"Are you ready to go back?" he asked.

"I guess."

"It was good having you home for a week. I hope you got some rest."

"I did."

He nodded and turned onto the road that went behind the dorms. I peered out my window, searching the square for friends.

"You know, James," he said, after a moment. "You and your mom are a lot alike."

I scoffed, but he didn't appear to notice.

"Both of you are dreamers," he continued. "You always want something better out of life. Bigger and better. The problem is, you don't see what you already have."

The Cricket Man of Dingo Wing

DICKIE WADED THROUGH A FLOOD of Styrofoam packing peanuts to help me with my bags. "Welcome back," he said.

I stared at the drifts of Styrofoam that covered our floor. "I love what you've done to the place."

"Courtesy of the Steves," he explained. "It was like this when I arrived half an hour ago."

Styrofoam peanuts squeaked beneath my shoes and clung to my legs as I shuffled to my bed. "Home, sweet home," I quipped.

We spent an hour picking up Styrofoam. Dickie acted like it was a huge pain in the ass, but I didn't mind. We chucked Styrofoam at each other until it speckled our hair and stuck to our faces. For a while, it was almost like old times, then Dickie noticed Styrofoam all over the tux he'd brought back for the Spring Fling and he freaked.

"Craptastic," he said, shaking the white crumbs off the inside of the garment bag. The more he tried to brush it clean, the more staticky it became.

"So you're taking Sunny to the Fling?" I asked.

"Uh-huh." He tore off the garment bag and shook out the tux.

"What do you plan on doing?"

"Nothing fancy." Styrofoam peppered the black lapels.

"Are you going to a restaurant?"

Dickie nodded. "Some Italian place. Heinous's dad hired a limo to take us—"

"Hold up," I interrupted. "Heinous has a date?"

"Dude, where've you been? Vanessa Drevadi and him are joined at the hip."

"Wow. The pigs are flying."

"Anyhow," Dickie continued, "Amber Lane is having a party, so we might leave the dance early and go there. Her parents are out of town. She lives in this mansion with an indoor pool, and she's letting people stay the night."

"A pool, eh? Sounds fun."

That was the signal for Dickie to invite me along. *There's always room for one more,* he could say. *Amber wouldn't care. We've rented a limo, for Christ's sake, so you have to come. The Three Amigos ride again!*

But he didn't say any of that. Instead, he pulled the garment bag back over the tux and kicked some remaining Styrofoam peanuts under the bed. "It'll probably be lame," he muttered. "I didn't think you'd be interested. I mean, you're not going to the Fling, are you?"

"Bloody hell," I said, forcing a British accent. "Could you picture me in a flippin' tux?"

Dickie grinned. "I doubt the DJ would play any Sex Pistols."

"No one respects the classics."

"I mean, what would Sid Vicious do?"

"Probably vomit on the chaperones."

"So you're cool?" he asked.

"Definitely."

"Right-o." Dickie grew silent, looking at his tux again. "I think I'm going to see who else is back."

"Never mind the bollocks," I replied.

"Huh?"

"It's from a Sex Pistol's album."

"Oh. I'll see you later."

"Right-o," I said.

I finished picking up the rest of the Styrofoam alone, then decided to call it a night. It wasn't until I turned off the lights and went to bed that I discovered the true genius of the prank.

Crickets.

Three seconds after I closed my eyes, the place chirped like a meadow in heat. Crickets trilled from beneath my bed, under the desk, behind the closet, even the bathroom. I flicked on the light and tried to catch them, but they were impossible to find. After twenty minutes of searching, I finally gave up and crawled back to bed.

I couldn't risk earplugs again, so I shut my eyes and pretended I was camping.

If Dickie did something to the Steves in retaliation, he never told me about it. I suppose that was for the best since I couldn't risk getting in any more trouble. I started to like the sound of the crickets, anyway. Dickie borrowed the custodian's industrial strength Shop-Vac and tried to suck them off the floor, but the little guys must have buckled down into cracks or held on to the carpeting, because they didn't go away. Eventually, Dickie gave up and dragged his mattress to Heinous and Cheese's room to sleep there.

Left alone in the room, I became the Cricket Man of Dingo Wing. I put pieces of bread and lettuce under my bed in case the little guys got hungry. I even named a few, based on their different locations. There was Sid, after Sid Vicious, since he lived somewhere near my Sex Pistols poster. And Krishna, who hung out around my ramen stash. And Lu-Lu the Wailer, who lived beneath my bed. It's not like I'd completely flipped and talked to the crickets all day, but they kept me company. No wonder I couldn't get a date.

As the weather warmed, people started going outside again for social hour. I made it part of my schedule to stroll around campus from ten to ten thirty. Usually,

I avoided the crowds and wandered around the pond. That's where I found Jess one night, pacing behind a hill, sneaking a cigarette.

"Howdy, stranger," I said. We hadn't spoken all semester—not since the night she'd visited my hometown.

"Howdy, asshole," she replied.

"I'm getting this weird vibe that you're pissed at me."

She took a drag of her cigarette, keeping her hand cupped to hide the cherry. "I was pissed."

"And now?"

She shrugged. "Guess I can only hold a grudge for so long. You might have outlasted it."

"Sorry," I said. "You know, about acting crazy and driving your dad's car off the road."

"Could have told me that before."

"Better late than never, right?"

She flicked some ash off the end of her cigarette, kicking a spark as it fell. Leather boots, fishnets, and black skirt—classic Jess. Her shirt was cut low, revealing the lines of her tattoo on her chest. I tried not to stare, but it still entranced me.

"Hey," I asked, "are you going to the Fling with anyone?"

"Don't start with me, bub."

"What? I'm asking as a friend. We can be friends, right?"

"I don't know. *Can we?*" There was an angry edge to her voice. I hadn't realized how much I must have hurt her. No one had ever liked me enough to get hurt by me before.

"I was kind of a jerk. Wasn't I?"

"I always fall for jerks," she said.

"You deserve better."

Jess took a long drag, narrowing her eyes as she exhaled. "Look, I just got over you, so you're not allowed to be sweet, okay?"

"Okay." I took a step back, raising my hands in surrender. "I won't be sweet. Scout's honor."

She chuckled.

"Besides," I added, "I think I'm cursed to be alone right now."

She gave me a long look. "You all right, J.T.?"

"Yeah. I'm fine," I said, surprised that she still worried about me.

"I heard you got in a fight with a window."

"We had a little disagreement about reality."

Jess smirked. "I should probably head in."

I didn't want her to leave yet. "I still have your flask," I said. "It's in my room. I could drop it by your dorm sometime if you'd like."

"Keep it. It was a gift."

"You sure?"

"Something to remember me by."

"Thanks."

She turned and started to walk toward her dorm.

"Wait. Can I ask you a question?"

Jess paused.

"What does your tattoo mean?"

"You're asking me that *now*? It's a bit late, don't you think?"

She had a point. Why hadn't I tried to know her better when I was with her? It was like what my dad had said—I never noticed what I had. "Please. I really want to know."

She glanced at her dorm, then at me. "It's from a poem by Matsuo Bashō," she finally said. "In Japanese it reads *Yume wa kareno o.*"

"You know Japanese?"

"I'm learning to speak it. I want to go there after I graduate."

"I didn't know that."

"There's a lot about me you don't know." She brushed her fingers across the top two characters of the tattoo. "Anyhow, this is the middle line from Bashō's last poem. His death poem."

"What's it say?"

"It's hard to translate." She kept her hand over her chest, protectively. "Pretty much, it says, *My dream goes wandering.* Or *In dreams I wander.*"

I stood, wondering about all the things I didn't know about Jess.

"What?" she asked.

"I like it," I said. "It's pretty."

Jess frowned. "I told you, *don't be sweet.*"

"Right. Sorry."

She glanced at her dorm again. "I better go."

"Take care, Jess."

"You, too. No more fighting windows."

"Hey, I learned my lesson. I'm good now."

"I doubt that," she replied.

I gave her a puzzled look.

"Just watch out for yourself," she said, and walked away.

The Fling

I FOUND A DATE. With Ariel. Okay, she had fins instead of feet, but she sure looked cute in her shells. The best part was I didn't even need to buy tickets to the Fling or splurge for dinner. Ariel preferred sitting in the commons and singing songs with me, and boy could she sing.

Unfortunately, the chess club had reserved the dorm DVD for a Friday night sci-fi movie fest. The only guys attending were Jesus John and Roger Herkle. They were too wrapped up in debating the weapons capabilities of various starships to hear my impassioned arguments for watching *The Little Mermaid.* Not only had it been my favorite movie as a kid, but it was the only DVD available from our wing library that wasn't scratched beyond viewing.

Ariel and I decided to move our shindig to the girls' dorm. I even dressed up for the occasion—putting on my best sport coat and ripped jeans. I mussed my hair into a respectable purple tangle, grabbed my seven iron to use as a cane (my five iron was in the pond), and, with Ariel under my arm and a bag of microwave popcorn, headed off.

The girls' dorm bustled with activity. A few guys, looking stiff in their tuxes, hung around the commons, waiting for their dates. Packs of girls darted from wing to wing, fixing each other's hair, trading jewelry, doing makeup. Some looked so different dressed up that I didn't recognize them, but not even the prettiest off-the-shoulder dress could compete with seashells. Another plus for Ariel, the wonder date.

Frank Wood saw me in my digs and asked who I was going with.

"Ariel," I said.

His forehead wrinkled. I could see him scanning a mental list of all the girls in school.

"The flipper thing's kind of a drag," I added. "She can't dance very well on land, but under the sea—look out!"

Frank noticed the movie. Then he got it. "Oh," he said.

I explained how I liked flipper Ariel more than legged Ariel. "She was more daring and adventurous with flippers," I told him. "With legs, she only cared about kissing Prince Eric. Now he's a total trog. Once they split, I'm going to swoop in and Ariel will be mine."

"Right," Frank said, backing away. "That's funny."

I grinned, although I wasn't entirely joking. The truth is, I've always been a little obsessed with cartoon women.

Frank's date came down, and he struggled with pinning a corsage to her dress. It took him almost five minutes to get it to stay on. Then they headed out, leaving me alone with Ariel again.

I started to imagine what Chuck would say about my cartoon crushes. He'd probably call it "a manifestation of my desire for an unattainable ideal."

"Why would I want someone who's unattainable?" I thought, carrying on the conversation in my head.

"I don't know," imaginary Chuck replied. "Why *would* you want someone who's unattainable?" (Half the time, all he did was repeat my questions back to me.)

"Because they're safe."

"Exactly," he said. "Real people are unpredictable. They might get angry at you. They might ignore you. They might reject you when you ask them to a dance. . . ."

I shook my head, snapping out of the imagined conversation. This was the problem with being alone too much—I'd get lost in my own thoughts. I hoped no one had noticed me spacing out. Glancing around, I tried to see if any friends had entered the commons.

Kevin Heegan and a few seniors were standing by the vending machines. While most guys pretty much swam in their tuxes, Heegan, with his broad chest and big shoulders, fit his perfectly. His hair was gelled into neat spikes, and he carried a bouquet of red roses. Ice Queen and he would look so dashing together—two blond, blue-eyed models.

Heegan's woodchuck laughter reverberated off the walls as he clowned around with his jeek buddies. I cranked up Ariel to drown him out.

Dickie and Heinous walked in a few minutes later. "Howdy, mates!" I called.

They strolled over. Heinous looked like an Elvis impersonator in his white tux.

"Going to Vegas?" I asked.

"Vegas?" Heinous said.

"Your tux, man. It's like you're going to get married."

"It's classic," Dickie said, although he was sporting a more traditional black tux himself.

"Classic '80s," I quipped.

"Dude." Heinous shook his head. "Real men wear white."

"And cummerbunds," Dickie added, pointing to Heinous's waist. "He's even wearing a cummerbund."

"James Bond wears a cummerbund," Heinous said. "Matadors wear cummerbunds."

"Cummer what?"

"The *cummerbund*," Heinous said, unbuttoning his jacket to show off the black sash around his waist. "Women love cummerbunds."

I tried to keep joking about cummerbunds with Dickie and Heinous, but they got distracted by the door opening. Sunny and Vanessa entered, and the couples went all gaga, complimenting each other.

In truth, Sunny did look pretty stunning. She had on this peach flowy dress with sparkles in her hair and glitter on her chest that made her tan skin shimmer. "You sure do clean up nice," I said.

"Thanks," she replied, nodding to my ripped jeans. "So do you."

They hung around the sofa, but I could tell they didn't want to spend too long in my pity fest. Heinous kept glancing out the window for the limo.

"Put a limo up your butt," I said.

His brow creased.

"Remember? That Eddie Murphy song . . ." I explained, but it was pointless—Heinous was too caught up in trying to impress Vanessa to sing a song about shoving things up one's buttocks.

More girls poured into the commons, all spiffed up. Sage Fisher. Jen Hinky. Rachel Chang. And Ellie.

The stomach-go-flip feeling I always got when she was around nearly floored me. Ellie had on this simple red dress, but the way it hung off her waifish figure made the other girls look like they were only playing dress-up. It seemed impossible that she could be one of us and not some magazine picture come to life. For a moment, I was as intimidated by her as ever, then her eyes found mine and her composure faltered. I knew she hadn't meant to look at me. She probably hadn't expected me to be there.

The crack in her armor lasted only a fraction of a second before she regained her composure. Her high heels clicked against the tile floor as she walked toward me. I froze, trying to still my spinning insides. The notion that she might give me a second chance flitted through my head. I imagined her whispering something cheesy like, "I'll save a dance for you," then I'd go to the Fling and by the end of the night we'd be laughing about all the dumb things that had kept us apart.

Instead, she breezed past the couch as if I didn't exist. Heegan stood behind me. Ellie thanked him for the flowers and complimented his tux.

I stared at the TV. Ariel was twirling in her secret cove, singing about how she wanted to be part of the human world.

When next I looked, Heegan and Ellie were gone. They must have slipped out the back of the commons. Then the limo arrived, and Heinous, Vanessa, and Dickie headed for the door. Sunny paused by my couch before leaving.

"You going to be okay?" she asked.

"Yeah. I've got popcorn and Ariel. What more could a guy want?"

She looked at me like she thought I might slit my wrists or jump off the roof.

"I'm fine," I added. "Really. Have fun at the dance. Don't do anything I wouldn't do."

Sunny smiled. "That pretty much leaves it open, doesn't it?"

The Girl Who Had Everything

"I'M FINE," I TOLD CHUCK. "I've got everything under control."

"I see." He folded his hands beneath his chin, giving me this attentive one-eyed look, like a compassionate pirate.

Chuck usually let me pick whatever I wanted to talk about, but this time I couldn't come up with a thing. All week my mind had been totally blank.

I leaned forward and grabbed the paperweight from the table. It was one of those handblown glass balls with bright swirls and bubbles in the middle. Looking at it reminded me of the sparks trapped in jars that I'd seen in the core.

"You know," I said, "I don't think I need to come here anymore. I think I made up all my problems."

"It doesn't seem that way to me," Chuck said.

"Whatever." I hadn't cut myself. I hadn't dreamed of the city. I hadn't done anything bad in weeks. "I think I'm cured. I'm fine now." I pulled back my sleeves as proof. "Model citizen."

"Do you feel fine?"

"Yeah."

"What's that feel like?"

"Nothing," I said. "Like tasting water."

Chuck stared, waiting for me to say something more.

I glanced around the room. The clock on the bookshelf had stopped. I wondered if Ellie was sitting outside the office yet, eager to start her session. We had this tacit system where I'd bolt out of the office and she'd pretend to be so involved in reading a magazine that she wouldn't look at me. It was like running through a cold sprinkler, except after my last meeting she hadn't been there.

"Did Ellie stop seeing you?" I asked, figuring Chuck wouldn't answer. There was probably a rule against talking about other students.

"Why do you ask? Are you friends with her?"

"Sort of." It seemed too complicated to explain that Ellie and I were only friends before I knew it was her. "We used to be very close."

Chuck rubbed his hands together in thought. "Hold on a second. I need to make a phone call."

He left me in his office for almost five minutes before he stuck his head back in. "Let's do something different today," he said, grabbing his coat. "How about a field trip?"

I shrugged. "Where to?"

"The hospital," Chuck said.

"Why?"

"To see Ellie."

Chuck signed me out. He drove this tiny compact car that creaked when he got in. His head almost touched the ceiling and his knees jammed around the steering wheel. The car was cluttered with trash and sunflower seeds. Chuck swiped a coffee cup off the seat and straightened this green towel where I was supposed to sit. Short white hairs covered every inch of the car.

"Sorry about the dog hair," he said.

"No problem," I told him, cramming into the seat.

We didn't talk much on the way. I asked Chuck what Ellie was doing in the hospital, but the only answer he gave me was, "You should ask her that."

Fortunately, the hospital wasn't very far away. It was the same place the ambulance had taken me when I got hypothermia, only it looked different now in daylight and without snow.

Inside, the place appeared plenty familiar—harsh white lights, antiseptic smell, and bodies bustling in blue scrubs. Chuck talked with a nurse at the front desk, then he led me through the maze of hallways to Ellie's room. A few of the doors we passed stood open. In one, a gray-skinned old man lay among a nest of IV tubes, beeping machines, and ventilator hoses. In another room, a middle-aged woman in a hospital robe sat upright in bed, eyes glued to a TV that hung from the ceiling. Wilting flowers and balloons surrounded her. I got nervous thinking about what the situation in Ellie's room might be.

Chuck knocked twice on a door that was cracked open. "You decent?" he called.

No one responded.

"Go on," he said to me. "She knows you're coming."

I looked at him, still not sure what I was supposed to do, but he didn't give me any more instructions. Chuck was big on letting people figure things out for themselves. I took a deep breath and pushed open the door.

A dull yellow curtain surrounded the bed like a cocoon, through which I could see the muted glow of a reading lamp.

"I'll be in the waiting room," Chuck said. "I've got thirty minutes before I need to return to school. All right?"

"Sure." I stared at the yellow curtain surrounding Ellie's bed. It made me think of the pod in the center of the core where I'd left the Thief, surrounded by Nomanchulators. My stomach knotted.

Chuck squeezed my shoulder and headed off. I listened to his footsteps recede.

"Can I come in?" I asked, breaking the silence.

"If you want to," Ellie replied. Covers rustled as she moved about.

I parted the curtain and stepped through.

Ellie sat among several pillows with her legs crooked

beneath a blanket. She had a hair band in her mouth and she struggled to put her straight blond hair back in a ponytail, only it was too short so it kept slipping free. She gave up finally, leaving half her hair pulled back while the other half brushed her cheek. "I've got bed-head," she muttered.

"You look great," I said, my voice wavering. Shadows underlined her eyes and her skin was sallow.

Ellie scoffed.

"You do," I added, trying to cover up my shock at how different she seemed. "It's good to see you."

"Please. I can tell when you're lying."

I took a step back and considered leaving. Obviously, she didn't want me there, but if I left now, I might hurt her feelings again. I didn't want her to know how much it bothered me to see her like this.

"So, how's it going?" I asked, attempting to play it cool.

Ellie didn't respond.

I searched the room for something else to talk about. An IV hung next to her bed, but there were no beeping machines or ventilators. There were no flowers or balloons, either. I wondered if she'd had any visitors. Chuck probably thought I'd cheer her up. I should have told him that Ellie hated me.

"You want to hear something funny?" I asked.

Her eyes flicked over me but she still didn't talk.

"In the emergency waiting room, we passed this guy with a two-by-four nailed to his foot." I held up my hands to show how long the board was. "No kidding. He shot a nail straight through his foot, boot and all, and into a block of wood."

"That's not funny."

"Guess you had to see it. He seemed pretty embarrassed."

Ellie fidgeted with the blanket, smoothing out the wrinkles over her legs. I stuck my hands in my pockets, hoping she'd say something to end the awkwardness, but she didn't.

"Why are you here?" I finally asked.

"Isn't it obvious?"

I looked at her sunken cheeks and thin arms. It *was* obvious, but that didn't explain why. I shook my head.

"What are people saying about me at school?"

"Nothing," I said, leaving off the fact that almost no one talked to me anymore.

"Oh." She stared at the blanket. "Well, I passed out."

"Why?"

"Low blood sugar, I suppose. The doctor said my electrolytes were so out of balance that I could have gone into cardiac arrest. That's why they kept me this time."

"You have heart problems?"

"Not exactly." Her hands kept fidgeting with the blanket, twisting a loose thread around her finger. "It's what happens when you only eat toast and lettuce for long enough. Your body starts to feed off itself. First the fat, then your muscles and joints. Then your brain can't regulate things. Bones deteriorate. . . . Pretty, huh?"

I glanced around the room, unable to meet her gaze. An orange cafeteria tray sat on a rolling cart near the side of her bed. It had one of those metal covers on it—the sort butlers used in cartoons to keep food warm. The smell made me hungry. "At least the food here's probably better than ASMA's," I joked.

"Of course," Ellie said. "Everyone thinks it's so simple. All I have to do is eat a cinnamon roll or a hot dog and I'll be better, right?"

My face flushed. "It's not like you need to diet."

"Right. Because this is all about looking cute in a hospital gown."

"So why do you starve yourself?"

"Why do you cut yourself?" she countered.

I hesitated, stung by her question. "Okay," I admitted. "Maybe it's not so simple."

Ellie scooted over and moved her book—*The Bell Jar* by Sylvia Plath. "Here," she said. "You can sit."

I hoisted myself onto the bed, crossing my legs.

"Chuck says it's about control," she explained. "I can't control my life, so I try to control myself by not eating. And the worse I feel, the more I have to starve myself to be good. Or pure. Or worthy."

"Is that what you think?"

"Sometimes." She twisted the loose hospital band on

her arm. "The explanations don't really matter, though. They don't change anything. I'm still stuck in this cycle, wanting to be thin."

"But you are thin."

"I'm never thin enough," she said. "That's the problem."

I thought of all the things she'd written to me—about how she was consumed by image, and how she wanted to be a zero, as if disappearing was the only way to be perfect. She'd kept telling me that she could never be herself in person, but I was too blinded by what I wanted her to be to see what she was talking about. Only now, when I looked at her intense eyes and slender neck, and how lost her tiny arms seemed in the wide sleeves of her hospital gown, it was like some spell had finally broken. Her image dissolved, and I saw her true self—the ghost that was fading away.

"I'm sorry," I said.

"For what?"

"Sorry I said you were dead inside. I didn't mean it."

"Then why'd you say it?"

"Because I was afraid you'd see the truth about me."

Ellie studied me.

There was no point lying anymore—I'd already lost everything. "I'm not who people think I am," I said.

"Who is?"

"This is different. I lied to everyone about my past. The things I've done . . . Who I am . . . Everything about me is fake."

She grew silent, lost in thought for a moment. Then she nudged my leg. "Thank you."

"For being a massive jerk?"

"For being honest."

"But I'm not honest. That's what I'm telling you— I can't be honest. I don't even know what's real anymore." I picked at the hospital blanket, pulling off a fluff ball. "These last few weeks, I've been trying to act normal and fit in, only I can't do it right. Everyone takes it for granted that they're real, but I have to try to be real. And if you try to be real, what are you?"

"I know what you mean."

"You do?"

"I'm like that all the time," she said. "I'm constantly obsessing over how I should talk, or act, or eat—calculating the exact number of calories I need to cut to become this idea of who I'm supposed to be. I do it so often, I don't think there's anything real left underneath." She shrugged. "There's just this empty shell, pretending to be human."

"That's not true." I wished she could see herself the way I saw her—not some cold, distant model, but the girl who'd IM'd me and kept me from being alone. "You are the most sincere, passionate, real person I've ever met."

"I don't think that person exists anymore."

"She does," I said. "I'm talking to her."

Ellie grew silent, staring at her hands. I blew on the blanket fluff I'd pulled off and the tiny ball swirled into the air, landing in her lap. She picked it up and smiled shyly, as if I'd given her something precious and she feared she might lose it.

"*Smilet*," I said.

"Huh?"

"That's my favorite word. Not *ucalegon*. *Smilet*. It means half smile, only it's not really a word. I think Shakespeare made it up."

"I like it. It should be a word."

"As in," I added, "'You have the prettiest smilet in the world.'"

"Or, 'Wipe that smilet off your face!'"

She said it in such a mean voice that we both cracked up.

We talked for a little while after that about school, and our parents, and our hometowns, but we didn't have much time left before Chuck came to take me back.

Instead of saying good-bye, I pointed to a crease in the blanket between us.

"That's the gap," I said. Then I held out my hand and reached across.

Ellie reached back, wrapping her slender fingers around mine. "So are you disappointed that I'm not the perfect girl you thought I was?"

"No. I like you much better now—bed-head and all."

"You, too," she replied. "It's good to finally meet you, James."

Under Control

IT WASN'T ANYTHING LIKE normal sleep. I felt the familiar change happening, my mind descending into forbidden corridors. Again and again I went to sleep, diving deeper into darkness until I landed in the core. The mucky ground gripped my ankles, pulling at me with its promise of oblivion.

"You didn't need to come back here," Nick said. He leaned against the stone wall of the cavern, cradling a jar full of hundreds of glowing sparks. "There are no more demons. You've won."

I glanced around the cave. All the smaller jars were gone, leaving the wet stone walls drenched in shadow. In the center of the cavern stood the pod where my other self slept, like a great black heart surrounded by sticky cords. I certainly wouldn't miss this place. Still, something about what Nick had said didn't make sense. The last time I'd been here, things had gone horribly wrong. How could I have won?

"I don't get it," I said.

Nick held out the jar and shook it. The sparks swirled around, tinking against the glass. "The Thief." He grinned, flashing his perfect teeth. "She thought she had you, didn't she? But you weren't fooled. You tricked her."

I thought of how the Thief had sacrificed herself to save me. "I didn't mean to."

"Sure you didn't," Nick replied. "I knew, first time I saw you, you'd be the one to catch her. She was the last demon."

I rubbed my forehead. My face was covered, same as usual, with a scarf to hide my identity. From whom, I didn't know. The core appeared empty except for Nick and the jar cradled in his gloved hands.

"Where is she?" I asked.

"With the rest of them." Nick flicked the jar. Sparks scattered, hitting the glass and sliding into a glowing pile at the bottom. "This is it—all your problems."

I stepped closer to get a better look.

"The Thief was the one who kept letting the other demons out," he said. "She was the reason *some of them came back. It never would have ended as long as she was free."*

I nodded, recalling how she'd busied herself stealing jars when we were here before. At least that part of Nick's story fit.

"Can I see that?" I asked, reaching for the jar.

"Careful with it. They're angry buggers."

I cupped the jar and stared at the sparks. A few fluttered like lightning bugs, but most lay still at the bottom, their yellow glow growing dull. "She's in here?"

Nick nodded. "She won't be causing you any more trouble."

"Now what?" I asked, giving the jar a shake. Some sparks brightened momentarily.

"Now it's over. You've become what you wanted to be, and you don't have to worry about this mess anymore." Nick nodded to the jar. "It's all under control."

"Control," I repeated. The word tasted metallic. This was what I'd fought for. It felt so quiet. So dead.

I let the jar fall from my hands.

For one hushed moment it turned in the air in perfect silence. Then it exploded against the stone floor. Sparks swirled around me, expanding, filling the cavern with their angry buzzing. Several whirled off, landing at the base of the stone walls where they glowed like embers. Others shot past Nick and disappeared into the darkness.

"You shouldn't have done that," Nick said.

I watched the sparks. They pulsed and grew, becoming more solid, taking on hideous, familiar forms.

Nick backed away. "Better run."

Instinctively, I started for the elevator, then I saw the Thief crumpled near the base of the pod where my other self slept. I hurried to her side and tried to help her stand, but she was too weak.

Several demons around us had nearly re-formed. They stretched their limbs and licked their wounds, glaring at me as they regained strength.

"Leave," the Thief said.

I shook my head. "I'm not not running away anymore."

Demons hissed and growled as I stood. I drew my sword, but there were too many to fight. For the first time, I thought of surrender. It had never seemed like a choice before. Until now.

My hands shook as I laid my sword on the ground and turned my back on the demons. Stepping toward the pod, I reached to touch the sleeper within. Deep in that shadowy heart, I could barely make out his eyes moving beneath closed lids.

Several demons charged—flashes of move-
ment at the edge of my vision. They slammed into
me and pinned me against the pod wall. I opened
my mouth to scream but couldn't draw breath.
Claws tore at my gut and teeth pierced my neck.
Then a searing pain scorched through me and all
thought blazed out to an ashy darkness.

Spring

I CAME TO IN A FOREST. *Sunlight, the smell of pine trees, and the trill of crickets flooded my senses.*

"You're free," the Thief said. "You found a way out."

I felt my teeth with my tongue and touched my cheek. My face seemed to be there. My body intact, but different. Heavier. More present. "What happened?"

"You were eaten. Devoured, actually. It was pretty disgusting."

"Did I die?"

"Yes and no," she said. "Who you were died. Who you are is very much alive."

I tried to piece together my memories. Some images came to me as if I'd been standing before myself, watching my body get torn apart, except it wasn't exactly scary. From where I'd stood, it seemed like the demons weren't attacking me—they were *me. They'd been part of me all along, only my fear hadn't let me see it. They were the things I'd tried to cut away from myself. The parts I wouldn't allow or couldn't accept.*

"You were broken," the Thief said. "Now you're whole."

"I don't feel whole. I hurt. I'm confused. Scared..."

"Wonderful, isn't it? To feel so many things again."

I squinted at her. All at once, I realized whose perspective I'd seen myself from. "The other—am I him?"

"Are you the dreamer or the dream?" the Thief replied. She smiled and kissed my forehead. "Perhaps you're both."

When I woke in my dorm, everything wasn't better. It wasn't easy like that. There was no magic potion to make me right. Instead, I ached. Deeply. I thought of Ellie, Jess, Moms, Dickie, the school year ending, the trill of crickets in the morning light, and I cried. I wasn't even sad. It was more like I cried for the people I'd miss and the wonder and beauty in the world—all the things I'd lost, and all the things to come.

Maybe I only cried because I wanted to. Still, it felt real, and that was a start.

Yearbook

THE LAST DAY OF SCHOOL, there weren't any classes or finals or anything. We were supposed to pack our stuff and clean out our dorm rooms. My parents were coming that evening to pick me up. I'd called them a few days before to arrange things, which pretty much stunned my mother speechless. It might have been the only time I'd ever called them first. It's not like I was looking forward to spending the summer at home, but I'd decided to declare a truce with my mom and try to accept her for who she was with the hope that she might do the same for me. To her credit, she said I sounded good on the phone. Then Dad said he was proud of me for finishing the semester.

I'd packed most of my things that morning, except for my posters, which I wanted to keep up until the last minute since bare walls depressed me. I probably should have spent the afternoon cleaning—the crickets still owned my room, and there were bits of moldy bread and rotting lettuce under the bed—but everyone else was at the square signing yearbooks and I didn't want to miss out.

I wandered campus, trading my yearbook with people, even people I hadn't been friends with. The hard part was that every time I asked someone to sign my book, they asked me to sign theirs, and I couldn't think of what to write.

Some people signed next to their pictures, adding a funny word bubble to candid shots of them at the dance or studying in their dorms. There was only one candid shot of me in the yearbook, though, and I didn't want to sign next to it. I kind of wished it wasn't in the book at all.

The picture was of me after the ultimate freak. My head lay cocked to the side, purple hair in a crazy tangle, eyes half shut, and tongue lolling out the side of my mouth. One arm clenched my chest while the other hung limp near Jess's feet. Ketchup splotches covered my shirt, but since the picture was black and white, it looked more like grease stains than blood.

People kept saying to me, "Nice picture, J.T." Then they'd nod and smile, or wink or something, like they wanted me to know they were in on the joke.

No matter how many times I looked at the picture, I didn't recognize it as myself. I mean the T-shirt, ripped jeans, and wild hair—it all looked like me, and I remembered lying there. Except the person I'd been then seemed strange to me now.

The old me would have dissed the whole yearbook-signing thing. Or if I did sign someone's yearbook, I would have written something ridiculous, like:

I'm just glad to be here. —John Lennon

or

Next year I'm going to kick your ass!
—Mahatma Gandhi

Now, I took it seriously. A few times, I even snuck off to see what people had written in my book. Mostly it was lame, shallow stuff:

You're a noble adversary, but you cannot defeat the power of Steve squared. Chirp, chirp! Steve squared wins again.

Put sophomore year up your butt, baby! We rule! —Heinous Man

Good luck with Ariel. You're one strange cat. Try not to burn down your house over the summer. —Frank Wood

Eat me! —Rachel Chang

Dear Man of Mystery. Soon you shall have the power to drive (legally). Very scary. I wish I'd gotten to know you better. Next year we should go bowling together. —Sage Fisher

Here's an equation for you. Zaftig hottie + my head = OOO (I'm the one in the middle). Keep the lamp on and the moths will come. Mmmm . . . Cheese

Stay cool, dude. Don't jump out any more windows. I hear flying's overrated. —Dickie Lang

I don't know what I was looking for in people's messages. Some sense of who I was, maybe? I even asked Ralph, aka Muppet, to sign my book. He wrote, *I'm glad you didn't get kicked out. Next year I hope we can be physics partners again.* When I read that, I got so choked up I nearly lost it.

Ellie had come back from the hospital a few days before to finish the semester. I kept an eye out for her as I wandered around campus, but I didn't see her. No one I spoke with had seen her, either. Eventually, I got a pass to her wing and knocked on her door.

Her roommate had already left, so Ellie was alone, packing her things. The walls were totally blank, and most of her stuff sat in boxes. One of the boxes near the door was filled with textbooks I'd already returned. The teachers probably gave Ellie an extension on finals. I felt bad for her, knowing how hard it was to have work left to do when everyone else was done.

"Hey," I said, "want to sign my yearbook?"

She gave me a funny look and kept folding her shirts, getting the creases perfect before she set them in her suitcase. "Why? Are you going for a record? Amber Lane already has 102 signatures—some steep competition there."

"I prefer quality over quantity." I handed her my yearbook. "Tell you what, I'll even sign yours. And I'm picky about this sort of thing. Amber Lane would kill for my autograph."

"Is that so?"

"Okay. So maybe she didn't ask me. But that only makes me more of a rarity."

Ellie flipped through my book, looking for a blank spot. "Mine's on my desk," she said.

I sat on her desk and opened her yearbook. Every page I turned to was completely blank. I was the first person to sign it.

"You have to promise not to read what I write until you get home," she said.

"Sure."

"Promise?"

"Yeah. I promise."

She smiled and went back to writing.

I tried to come up with something heartfelt and witty to put in her book, but I couldn't think of a thing. Eventually, I scrawled a few lines about how we should write each other old-fashioned letters every day over the summer, and I couldn't wait to see her next year. Then it hit me why her book was blank. "Are you coming back next year?"

"I don't know," she said. "Depends how things go over the summer. My mom thinks the cafeteria food is why I don't eat. I keep telling her that I really like pancake enchiladas, but she doesn't believe me. She wants me to be closer to home so she can keep an eye on me, which means my dad wants me to be closer to him, so he can prove that he's the better parent." She tapped the pen against her lips. "What about you? Are you coming back?"

I gestured to the open book in my lap. "I already signed a dozen yearbooks with 'see you next year,' and I've got this new policy about always telling the truth."

"Good luck."

"No kidding." I flipped through her book, past the picture of me pretending to be dead. "I've told so many stories, it's hard to know what's true anymore."

Ellie shook her head. "I mean good luck being here."

"Oh." I set her yearbook down and looked out her window. She had a nice view of the main square where people gathered. "It's strange," I said. "I know most people can't wait for summer, but I wish I could stay here. I'm such a geek."

"No, you're not."

"What am I, then?"

"You, James Turner, are a baby. And I mean that in the very best way."

"Right. Because guys love to be called babies."

"The only real friends I've ever had were babies," she said, handing my yearbook back to me. "It means you're new. You're discovering things. We both are." Ellie leaned against the desk where I sat, fitting her legs between mine.

"So I'm your friend?" I asked.

"Uh-huh."

"A real friend?"

"You feel pretty real to me," she said, putting her hands on my shoulders. "You're not a ghost anymore."

I wrapped my arms around her waist.

For a moment, I thought I'd imagined the brush of her lips on my cheek, because I'd wanted so badly to kiss her. Then Ellie kissed me again, and this time our lips met. It was wonderful and sad—a hello and good-bye and everything else in one gesture. I kept thinking *This . . . this . . . this . . .* because it seemed incredible that I could be myself, and life could be this amazing.

"I'll write you," I said, pulling her so close I could feel her heart beating against my chest.

"You better," she whispered.

EPILOGUE

Dear James,

I'm looking at you right now, and there are so many things I want to tell you. That you scare me. That seeing your scars helps me to see mine. That you bring me back to myself. That because I met you, I want to stay. That I understand how fake words often sound, and how truth can swim beneath them like fish in an ice-covered lake. That I know who you are, and I think you know who I am, too.

Basically, I'm in syzygy with you.

Love,
Ghost44
P.S. Sweet dreams.

ACKNOWLEDGMENTS

Piece of Cake — that's what I thought when I finished the first draft of this novel. I've since been humbled. It took me four years and over a dozen rewrites to figure these characters out and unearth their secrets. Here's to the people who believed in this book and kept me going.

I especially want to thank:

My wife, Kerri, for reading this book nearly as much as I did, and being the one I always write for.

Lauren Myracle, Laura Resau, Ellie Echo, Trevor Jackson, my sister, Jill Mitchell, and The Minions (Steve Church, Abe Brennan, Sophie Beck, Jamie Kembrey, Emily Wortman-Wonder, and Oz Spies) for giving this manuscript early reads and excellent suggestions. Alvero, for pointing out that there needed to be a kiss. And David Levithan and Wendy Lamb for giving me expert advice.

Jennifer Yoon, for being a brilliant editor who stuck with me through more drafts than I care to remember. Amy Maffei, for looking up the ingredients in Chunky Monkey ice cream. James Weinberg for excellent design work. Deborah Wayshak, Elizabeth Bicknell, and all the other fine people at Candlewick, for helping a bunch of pages become a book.

Ginger Knowlton, the best agent ever, for believing in me. And Tracy Marchini, for staying in touch.

Heather Standley Hayward, for helping me remember things, and for never forgetting my birthday. Dickie and Heinous, for letting me borrow their nicknames. Ellen Landers, for inspiring me to take the writer's path. Justin Jesty, for Japanese translation help and ongoing friendship.

Hundreds of students in schools I visited for giving me title advice (I like *Syzygy*, too).

My family, for always supporting me. (No, I wasn't like James in high school. Really.) And my daughters, Addison and Cailin (who was born while I was finishing this) for waking me up early in the morning and reminding me of what's important.

Finally, I want to thank the faculty, students, and staff at the Illinois Mathematics and Science Academy — the school that changed my life.